SERAFINA'S PROMISE

A NOVEL

IN VERSE

BY ANN E. BURG

SCHOLASTIC PRESS ✳ NEW YORK

PART

ONE

Under my bare feet,
brown, brittle grass
prickles and stings.
Bubbles of dirt
crumble and snap.

Slowly, carefully,
I climb the dusty hill
like Gogo taught me—

One foot forward—
stop.
The other foot forward—
stop.

I stretch out my left arm.
My right hand
hovers close to my head,
ready to catch the bucket
if it tips or slides.

Slowly, steadily,
I climb and climb,
careful not to move my head.
Careful not to spill
the smallest drop of water.

✳
＊
＊

Twice a day,
I carry water
from the ravine
without spilling.

Each morning,
I sweep the floor
and empty
the chamber pots.

At night,
I pile charcoal
to make the cooking fire.

In August, Manman
will have her baby.

If I work hard
and help Manman,
maybe this time
our baby will live.

As I walk past the alley,
my best friends call to me,
Julie Marie and Nadia,
playful as children,
singing,
jumping rope,
laughing.

Julie Marie's brothers
Jacques and Daniel Louis
dart and dash
in crazy circles,
begging Banza,
our scraggly neighborhood dog,
to chase them.
Laughing and hooting,
they hide behind rusted barrels
and heaps of mud and garbage.

I wish I could
jump rope and laugh
with my friends.
But I have no brother
or sister to help with chores.
Even on Saturday,
there's no play
until all my work is done.

Mwen dwe travay, I call,
moving only my eyes.
I have work to do!

3

At the sound of my voice,
Banza runs to me.
His thin yellow body
nuzzles my leg.
I have nothing to give you,
Banza, I say,
still looking straight ahead.

Banza's mangy tail wags.
He trots beside me anyway.

✳

Banza is good company.
He listens to me sing
when I feel like singing,
and lets me grumble
when I feel like grumbling.
Manman tells me
to stay away
from the scabby dogs
that wander through
our neighborhood.
She calls them
unpredictable and *dangerous*.

But Banza isn't dangerous.
He's my friend.
Right, Banza? I say.
Ou se zanmi mwen.
You're my friend.

Banza nudges me
with his giant ginger-colored paw.

Manman doesn't understand.
She worries about everything.
Gogo tells me to be patient with her.
Papa says things will be different
when the baby comes.

Everything will be better
when the baby comes.

✳
 ✳
＊

Two more hills to climb.

I pass Julie Marie's house
and hear her manman singing.

Banza leaves me to explore
an abandoned cooking pit.
A heavy throbbing
sinks into my neck
and spreads
across my shoulders.
Gogo says, *Happy thoughts*
soothe aches better
than willow bark and clover.
So while I walk,
I think about tomorrow,
my favorite day.

On Sundays, Gogo helps me
with my chores.
On Sundays, Papa is home.
On Sundays, everyone parades
to the big white church
between the President's Palace
and Papa's supermarket,
where we all pray together.

I link arms with Nadia
and Julie Marie.
Behind us, grown-ups
carry babies and sing.

In church,
colors from the glass window
dance on my white skirt.
The priest kisses the altar
and sings, *Bondye bon!*

Bondye bon! we all sing.
We raise our arms
and clap our hands.
Bondye bon! God is good!

Beside me, Manman rubs her belly.
Her voice is low and sad.
Bondye bon, I pray.
Please let this baby live.

✳

Even colorful church thoughts
don't cheer me.
My arms are stiff with holding,
my mouth is dry as the dirt
under my feet.
The sun presses against my neck
like a burning rock.
One more hill, and I'll be home.
Beside me a row of thirsty shacks
leans against the mountain
like faded cardboard weeds.

Gogo says, *Weeds are flowers*
too poor for fancy clothes.

Just like me! I say.

Gogo shakes her head.
A kind heart
is the fanciest dress of all.
Gogo likes to talk in riddles.
She doesn't know
the bad feelings
that circle and bump
in my mind
like a swarm of angry bees.
She doesn't know
the secret swirling in my heart.

Only Julie Marie
knows my secret.

When I grow up,
I want to be a doctor
like Antoinette Solaine,
the woman with the red glasses
and the black bag
who tried to save Baby Pierre.

And to be a doctor,
I must go to school.

Julie Marie understands.
Julie Marie wants to be a doctor too.

Together we'll open a clinic.
We'll help the old people
who live too far from hospitals.
We'll care for hungry babies
too fragile and weak to survive.

But every day Gogo says,
Help your manman.
Every day Papa says,
Manman needs you.

How will I ever go to school
if I must always help Manman?

Nadia's mother has more babies
than Manman,
but while I go up and down,
back and forth

collecting water and gathering wood,
Nadia goes to school.

It's not fair.
How will I ever be a doctor
if there's no time for school?

✳

Yesterday at the ravine,
Nadia showed me and Julie Marie
her bright yellow notebook.

Be careful, don't touch!
she commanded.
She slid her delicate hands
across the shiny cover.
A sniffy smile spread
across her perfectly round face.
These are my French words.
Educated people speak French.

Something like rotten wood
burned in the hollow
of my stomach.
Nadia didn't notice.

Someday Serafina and I
will go to school too,
said Julie Marie.
She squeezed my hand.
Her dark eyes shined
like the seeds of the sapote fruit.
Tiny braids spiraled down
her forehead.
Papa says we look like sisters,
but Julie Marie is taller than me.
Her smile is wider than mine,
wider than the morning sky,
brighter than the white sun.

Well, the teacher gave me
the last yellow notebook,
Nadia said, holding hers
close to her heart.
The only ones left are gray.

Julie Marie smiled.
Outsides don't matter, she said.
What matters is on the inside.

Still, my chest burned
and my face felt stuck.

Gogo is waiting to wash the dishes,
I said, and raced up the hill.

✳

Speaking French
doesn't mean you're smart,
Gogo said when I told her
about Nadia and her notebook
and being educated.
The only real wisdom
is kindness.

I want to believe
what Gogo says,
but kindness alone
won't make me a doctor.

*　＊
　　＊
　＊

The first time I met Antoinette Solaine,
Pierre was only a few days old.
Thin, papery skin hung off his bones,
and he never cried.
Manman and I walked all morning
to bring him to a doctor.

When the sun was high in the sky,
we reached the white stone building
on the other side of the mountain,
down the hill from a great mango tree.
Manman unwrapped Pierre
and placed him on a long table.

A small, wiry woman
wearing a white coat
and red glasses greeted us.
Hello, my friends. Non mwen se
Antoinette Solaine.
She smiled when she talked,
and her voice rippled
like a bamboo flute.
She tugged a flattened silver bell
that hung from a pink tube
wrapped around her neck.
What have we here?
She pulled the tube apart,
stuck the ends into her ears,
and placed the silver bell
on Pierre's small chest.
Her dark eyes squinted.

Would you like to listen
to your brother's heart? she asked.

A gentle beat like a faraway drum
fluttered through the pink tubes.

Your brother's heart is very weak,
Antoinette Solaine said.
But we'll try to make it stronger.

✳

While Manman rewrapped Pierre,
Antoinette Solaine talked quietly.
If you don't eat, Pierre doesn't eat,
she said.

Manman looked down.
There isn't always enough food,
she whispered.

Antoinette Solaine turned to me.
Her voice was gentle but strong.
Whatever little you have,
make sure your manman takes
her fair share.

I thought of all the times
Manman had given me
an extra scoop of rice.
I'm not that hungry,
she always said.
She'd shake her head
and tell me to eat
so I could grow up healthy
and strong.

And when Papa brought home
the blackened fruit
that wouldn't sell
at the supermarket,
Manman would say,

Give it to Serafina.
She needs to eat more.

My stomach was always hungry
so I took it.
Was it my fault
that Pierre was so small and weak?

Was it my fault
that his bones were tiny twigs,
or that his heartbeat
was hollow and far away?

Two weeks later, Antoinette Solaine
visited us in a square white car
with dusty tires
and a red cross painted on the door.
I'm sorry I could not come sooner,
she said.
She brought us a fresh mango,
a package of rice,
and a sweet yam for Manman.

But it was too late.
Already we had wrapped Pierre
in a clean white cloth.
We had said prayers
and buried him in our yard.
Already Papa's mother and brother
had come with the priest
to cry with us
and mark Pierre's grave
with a cross made of stones.
Already Gogo had come
from her sister's house in Jacmel
to stay and comfort Manman.

Antoinette Solaine saw
the emptiness
in Manman's arms and eyes.
She held Manman's hand
and bowed her head.
Mwen regrèt sa, my friends,
I am so sorry.

✳

For a long while
we held hands in the quiet.
Big tears rolled
down Manman's cheeks.
Inside me,
something bruised
and broken
tumbled.
My whole body
felt hollow.

How could someone so small
leave so big a hole?

I couldn't help but wonder,
Was it my fault Pierre died?
If I had given Manman my rice,
would he have lived?

Finally,
Antoinette Solaine spoke.
I brought you a present,
she whispered.
She opened her black bag
and pulled out a flattened silver bell
attached to a frayed black tube.
The stethoscope is broken,
but you can pretend.

Through our tears,
Manman and I smiled.

I placed the silver bell
on Manman's chest
and listened.

In the quiet,
my own heart beat
its unspoken secret.
I promised myself
that one day
I would be a real doctor
like Antoinette Solaine.

＊

Sometimes I think
Papa already knows my secret.

One time when Manman
burned her hand cooking,
Papa watched me smash
a plantain leaf
and press it against her
blistered skin.
You have a gift,
he said, smiling at me.

When I bring home
an injured insect,
or pretend to use my stethoscope
on a wounded bird,
or when Papa catches me
sneaking food to Banza,
he laughs his rolling laugh
and says,
Your heart is too big
for your little body, Serafina.

He tilts his head and studies me.
Does Papa know my secret?
What would he say
if I told him?
Would he still say,
Help Manman.
Help Manman.
Help Manman!

✳
* ✳
  *

Manman, I'm here! I call
when I finally reach home.

Manman draws open
our flowered-sheet door
and steps outside.
She helps lower the bucket
onto a patch of packed dirt
outside our small wooden hut.

Wonderful! Manman smiles.
You're getting so strong!

Instantly the bees in my brain
turn to dust.

I follow Manman into
our front room.
An old tin table and a single
chair help prop up the slanted
wooden walls.
Three large pots and a stack
of dishes are piled in one corner.
In the other corner,
clean clothes hang neatly
across a stretch of tattered string.
In the back,
another sheet separates
one room into two,
a blanket on the floor
for Papa and Manman.

A blanket on the floor
for Gogo and me.

Nadia and Julie Marie
are jumping rope,
I say. *May I join them?*

Manman shakes her head.
I need you to gather more wood
and pile the charcoal.
Papa will be home soon.

Gogo comes in carrying the basket
of wild mint and thyme
she gathered from the field.

And we need you to help us
sort and bundle, Manman adds.

The bees in my brain wake up.

Maybe after din—
I hear Manman say,
but I'm already outside,
an angry buzz
roaring in my ears.

✳
✳
✳

When Papa comes home,
his strong arms
scoop me into the air.

Three leaves, three roots,
he sings.

In the tiny space
between the table and the beds,
we twirl and dip.

Papa's clean white shirt
billows as we turn.
My soft purple dress
floats and swirls.

To throw down is to forget.

Gogo sits in the doorway
brushing mud
from Papa's worn-out shoes.

Outside, Manman rests one hand
on her growing belly
as she stirs red beans and rice.

To gather up is to remember.

✳

When dinner is ready,
Gogo gives Manman the chair,
and we sit on the floor.

Flag Day is coming,
Papa says.
Let's all go to the city.

Louis! You know there is no time
for such things, Manman says.
Soon the baby will be here.
We need to work and save
as much as we can.

Papa shakes his head.
One day, Marie Rose.
One day to celebrate.

Non! We'll celebrate
when the baby comes.

All Manman wants to do is work.
Work, work, work.
She never wants to celebrate anything.

What about me? I say.
May I go to the city with Papa?
I promise to get extra wood
and extra water.
I'll get up extra early

to sweep the floors
and empty the chamber pots.

Papa's laugh is loud
and deep,
like rolling coconuts.
Manman just squints
and goes outside.

Please, Papa! I beg.
One day to celebrate?

✳

Enough, Serafina!
Papa scolds,
suddenly serious.
He follows Manman outside.

He'll change her mind.

Whenever Manman chides me
for hiding rice to feed Banza,
or spilling coffee on my white skirt,
Papa always intervenes.

She's still a child, he says.

She's eleven years old,
Manman argues.
But Papa has a way
of explaining things
so Manman understands.

When Papa talks,
the anger in Manman's eyes
softens
like stingers soaked in honey.

✳

The flag is not just a piece of cloth,
Gogo says as we scrub
and rinse the supper dishes.
The flag remembers
what the world forgets.
We were slaves, but now we're free.

Every year,
Gogo tells me the same thing.

The colors on the flag mean something.
Blue for hope.
Lespwa fè viv. Hope makes us live.
Red for blood.
Not just slave blood, but your blood,
the blood of Granpè.

Every year, I ask,
How did Granpè die?

Someday, when you're older,
Gogo always says.
Someday, I'll tell you.

✳

Gogo! I say.
Every day, twice a day,
I carry water from the ravine.
I sweep the floors
and gather charcoal.
Even Manman tells me
how strong I am.
When the baby comes,
I'll be a big sister.
You can tell me now, Gogo.
I'm old enough to know.

The gooey clouds that cover
Gogo's eyes flicker.
She dips the last dish
into the washbasin.
Her brown, wrinkled fingers
linger in the water.

Your granpè was a good man.
He took care of his family.
He tried to make a better life for us.

What happened?
I whisper.
Why is it such a secret?

He who gives the blow forgets,
Gogo says.
But he who carries the scar
remembers.

29

*
  *
 *

What happened, Gogo?
I ask again.

Gogo lifts the plate
from the water
and sits back on her heels.

We had a little garden
with vegetables and herbs,
and even some chickens.
Gogo smiles.
We were happy
building our life together.
Your manman was just
a little girl,
younger than you are now.
We minded our own business
and saved our money.
Granpè taught himself to read.
He wanted your manman
to go to school.

Granpè could read?

Wi! Your granpè could read.
He was teaching us to read too.
Education is the road to freedom,
Granpè said.

You know how to read?
Manman knows how to read?

Gogo shakes her head.
Non. We never had the chance.

She closes her eyes but I still
see them move
beneath her thin, powdery lids.

*I was finishing the supper dishes
just like today.
Your manman was sitting beside me
making cakes in the mud
and singing.
The sun was shining softly.*

*First we learn the letters,
Granpè said.
Then we learn the words.
He opened his book.
I set aside the last dish
and lifted your manman
onto my lap.
She was still singing
when we heard the shot—*

*and the piercing
squawk of a chicken.*

Gogo opens her eyes.
The Tonton Macoutes suddenly appeared
in our front yard.
I can still see them waving their long,
heavy machetes.
I can still see their straw hats
and dark glasses,
their blue shirts and belts made of guns
and bullets.
I can still hear them demanding
that we leave our land.

Take the chickens, your granpè said,
but this land belongs to my family.
I've read our history. I know my rights.
Every day your power fades.
The Tonton Macoutes grabbed him.
Your manman screamed
as we watched them
take Granpè away,
still clutching his book.

Gogo's eyes brim with tears.
I will never forget the sound
of my little girl's scream,
or the look on Granpè's face,
telling us to flee.

Gogo's voice flutters softly.
We left that same night.
We never saw Granpè again.

* *
*

Granpè was taken away
by the Tonton Macoutes?

Nadia told Julie Marie and me
terrible stories
about the Tonton Macoutes.

*They roamed the countryside
like evil bogeymen,* Nadia said,
her eyes bigger
than a tarantula's belly.
*The president and his son
gave the Tonton Macoutes power
to destroy anyone
who didn't agree with them.
The Tonton Macoutes
said they were keeping order,
but really they took people away
and killed them.*

When I got back
from the ravine that day,
I asked Manman about
the Tonton Macoutes.

She turned her head.
They are shadows now, she said,
her voice low and distant.
*Nadia should not even speak of them.
Neither should you.*

I didn't understand
why she sounded so sad.

I take Gogo's hand in mine.
Maybe Granpè came back.
Maybe he's looking for you still.

Gogo shakes her head.
The Tonton Macoutes never gave back.
They only took away.

She stands up and I know
there are no more questions.

Be patient with your manman, she says.
Her heart is full of fear.

✳

All night, I think about
Manman screaming
when the Tonton Macoutes
led her papa away.
Even when Manman is angry,
she never screams.
Did the Tonton Macoutes
take away Manman's voice
when they took away her papa?

Questions tumble
and tangle in my mind:

Why didn't Granpè give
the Tonton Macoutes
what they wanted?
If he had, would he still be here?
What good is being brave
if being brave gets you killed?
Which is better,
to tell the truth and die,
or to give the bad people
what they want and live?

I think about Granpè
wanting to educate himself,
wanting to educate his family.
If he were still here,
he would teach me to read.
He would tell Manman
that I should go to school!

Education is the road to freedom.
Doesn't Manman remember that?

I think of the silent promise
I made to myself
when I listened to Manman's heart
with my new stethoscope.
I make the same promise
to Granpè.

One day, I'll go to school
and learn to read
so I can become a doctor.
I won't forget you, Granpè.
I promise to find a way
to follow your dream.
I promise to make you proud.

✳

The sun is still buried
in darkness Monday
morning when I wake up.

I hear Papa
get ready for work.
Babay, Marie Rose,
mwen renmen ou,
he whispers.

Babay. I love you too,
she whispers back.

Their gentle voices are a lullaby
that soothes me back to sleep.

When I wake again,
Gogo's wrinkled fingers
peel a black banana.
Each of us takes half.
Manman nibbles yesterday's
beans and rice.

Then, when the sun
is just beginning to yawn,
we all get ready for work.

✳

Most days, Manman and Gogo
gather the wild mint and thyme
that grow along the hillside.
On Wednesdays and Fridays,
they travel to Port-au-Prince.
They sit on a corner
and sell their bundles.

My days are always the same.
Collect the water. Sweep the floor.
Empty the chamber pots.
Gather wood. Pile charcoal.
Collect more water.
But somehow,
today feels different.

Today,
new thoughts fill my mind.
New feelings press against my heart.

✳
  ✳

The morning walk
to the ravine
is quiet.
Only babies
and young children
sit on the road.
They suck their fingers,
and watch their mothers
hang wet clothes on frayed
pieces of rope.
Julie Marie's brother Michel
leans his brown,
swollen belly
against his mother's
stick-like legs.

Jacques and Daniel Louis
have already left to work
in the sugarcane fields.
Julie Marie is off
gathering branches
to make charcoal.
But lucky Nadia
sits in the bright yellow
mission house,
learning how scribbles make letters
and letters make words,
like the words we speak.

When you read,
you discover,

she says.
When you write,
you remember.

I think about Granpè.
I think about the promise
I made to him
and to myself.

I know I must talk to Papa.

✳

A quiet whimpering
distracts me from my thoughts.
Banza is curled at the ravine,
licking his paw.
I never see him
this early in the day.
Banza! I call.
He looks up
and limps toward me.

I put down my bucket
and pat his thin, bony back.
Did you get into a fight?

He crouches to lick his paw again,
and I kneel beside him.
Let me take a look at that.

His scraggy tail thumps softly
when I speak,
but he yelps when I touch
his swollen paw.
I let go,
put my hand under his chin,
and look into his large brown eyes.
Were you walking where
you shouldn't have been?
You need to be more careful.

Still talking, I take his paw
into my hand again.
In one swift movement,
I yank out a large, pointy thorn.

Banza yowls and jumps up.
Before he runs away,
he rewards me with
a soft look of gratitude
and a sloppy kiss.

Watch where you walk!
I call after him,
but he's already disappeared.

※

As the dark, cloudy water
flows into my bucket,
I wonder where Banza goes
when he disappears.
Sometimes we don't see him
for weeks.
I wonder what it's like
to always be hungry
and wander about every day
looking for food.

Sometimes I'm hungry.
Sometimes my belly
is so empty it grumbles,
and a plate of rice
or a black banana
is just not enough.
On those days,
Papa sings louder,
and Manman's eyes are softer.
Gogo takes my hand
and we dance away
the rumbles.

I wonder what hunger is like
without a family
to fill the emptiness.

I think about Baby Pierre.
He never had a chance
to grow fat with our love.

*
 * *
  *

When I return home,
I put down
the bucket of water
I collected,
and brush the dirt
from the stone cross
on Baby Pierre's grave.

In my mind,
I can still see his eyes,
darker than coffee beans.
I can still feel his body, so thin
I could count his bones.
I can still hear his heartbeat,
gentle as a faraway drum.

Gogo says spirits
are with us always.

Can you hear me, Pierre?
I whisper.
Even though
we only knew each other
a few weeks,
I miss you!
I won't ever forget you, Pierre.
I hope you're happy.
I hope you're not hungry.

I straighten the stones.

One day, I'm going to become
a doctor,
so babies like you
won't die anymore.

If you can,
please give me the courage
to talk to Papa
about going to school.

Babay, little brother,
I sing softly.
I will always love you.

✻

Manman and Gogo get home
before all my chores are done.
Already they've sold
everything they gathered.

Today was a good day,
Manman says.

Gogo's single white tooth
glistens in the sunlight.
*It's hard to believe
that it's already mid-May,*
she says, shaking her head.
*Flag Day isn't until Monday,
but people are already celebrating!*

An idea flutters into my brain
as if Granpè himself,
or maybe Baby Pierre,
is whispering in my ear.
Flag Day would be
the perfect time
to talk to Papa
about school.

I look at Manman.
She sees the question
in my face,
slowly tilts her head
and nods.
Wi, you may go.

But only if all your chores
are done!

Mèsi! Thank you!
Thank you! Thank you!
I knew Papa would change
Manman's mind.

I promise I'll get all my chores done
before Papa is ready to leave!

She laughs.
Well then, you'd better start now!

✳

When I see Papa coming
down the road,
I run to meet him.
He scoops me into his arms.

Manman said I could go!

Papa laughs.
She did? Well, I guess
that means you can!

I hug him tightly.
Mèsi, Papa!

He hugs me back.
Thank your manman,
not me.

He puts me down
and together we dance
all the way home.

✳

The next few mornings
creep slower than a snake in daylight.
The next few nights
drag longer than a monkey's tail.

Every minute
of every day,
I think about
the fun I'll have
in Port-au-Prince
on Flag Day.

Every minute
of every day,
I practice
what I'll say to Papa
about school.

Papa will smile
and listen to me
like he always does.

He'll nod and tell me
he's proud of me.

Then he'll say,
Let me think it over.

When he hears
how determined I am,
how could he say no?

✳

While Julie Marie and I
gather water,
I tell her my plan.

Julie Marie smiles
her big white smile.
*And don't forget to mention
how you took care of Banza's paw.
And how you already know
how to use a stethoscope
and how to count to five in French
like Nadia taught us.*

Don't tell Nadia yet, I say.
*She'll find a way
to spoil my plan.*

Julie Marie laughs.
No she won't — but I promise.

We carefully lift our buckets
onto our heads.

*I can't wait to hear
what your papa thinks,*
Julie Marie says.
Remember everything!

Hope and happiness
bubble in my heart.
Wi! I will!

Julie Marie smiles.
Uncle Bouki, Uncle Bouki,
she sings.
Are you sleeping? Are you sleeping?
My heart is close to bursting.

Get up to play the drum.
Get up to play the drum.

Flag Day is almost here.
There's so much to celebrate!

On Sunday night,
the tingling
in my stomach
makes it hard to sleep.

I wiggle and squirm
and beg Gogo
to tell me about Flag Day
when she was a little girl,
or about Granpè
and his books.

Shhhhh . . . Gogo says.
*A child who doesn't sleep at night
is a crocodile in the morning!*

✳

It's still dark
when Gogo pulls my toes.
Leve, Serafina!
she whispers. *Wake up!*

Tiny butterflies quiver
inside me—
no more waiting—
today is Flag Day!
I leap to do my chores.

Even in the blackness,
my feet easily follow
the curves and dips
that lead to the ravine.

I brush away the flies
and mosquitoes
and quickly fill my bucket
with black, still water.

When I get back,
Manman gives me
a small piece of bread.
I'm not hungry
but she'll make me eat,
so I push away the quivers
in three big bites.

Slow down, Manman says.
The city will wait.

I'll empty the chamber pots
and sweep the floors,
Gogo says.
Today is a day to celebrate.

Blue for hope.
Red for blood, I say,
hoping that Granpè
has been listening
to my prayers.

✳

Papa washes his face
while Manman ties
red and blue ribbons
in my hair.
Her hands work quickly.
It hurts when she tugs
my scalp,
but I don't complain.
Listen to your papa,
she says, *and remember,*
he has work to do before the parade.
Be patient and let him do his job.

Wi, Manman! I assure her.
I'll be patient!

Even on Flag Day
Papa must stack cans,
open boxes,
and pour bags of rice
into wooden barrels.
Gogo frowns.
The donkey sweats
so the horse
can be dressed in lace.
She gives me a pair of ragged shoes
patched with bark and straw.
The shoes are big for my feet
and the patches pinch and scratch.

Gogo! Papa says,
I am happy to have steady work!
André struggles every day.
I'm happy I can provide
food and clothes for my family.
He smiles at me.
I'm happy I could afford
ribbons for Serafina's hair.

André is Julie Marie's papa.
Even though there are days
when I hear
Julie Marie's stomach grumble,
even though Julie Marie
always wears a dress
too small for her long, skinny body,
even though I have *never* seen her
with ribbons in her hair,
Julie Marie is always smiling.
She never complains about anything.
When I think of Julie Marie,
I feel lucky to go to Papa's supermarket
and wait while he does his work.

Papa kisses Gogo and Manman
on both cheeks.
I do the same,
then take Papa's hand.

My heart beats faster
than a hummingbird's wing
as we step into the early
morning dark.

Together we follow the long,
winding road
that leads to the city.
Soon a shimmery pink light
appears in the distance.

Papa twirls me and smiles.
My little starlight dancer,
he whispers,
and all the words
I planned to say
flutter away.

✳

We walk through
my favorite field
of dry grass and pink flowers.
The scent of mango,
oranges, and wild thyme
wraps me in sweetness.
Manman calls this part
of our walk to the city
Haiti's piece of heaven.

Before long,
we pass the path
that leads to
Nadia's mission school.
My wishes and words
drift back.
I take a breath.
Papa, may I ask you something?

Papa looks at me and nods.
Wi, you may ask me anything.

But then, the smells change
to garbage, sweat,
and burning wood.
The fragrant field is gone.

Along the road,
huts made of straw
and rusted tin shacks
pile on one another.

They push away
my whiffling thoughts
and steal my courage.
Do you like parades
as much as I do?
I ask.

Papa shakes his head
and laughs his hearty laugh
as the sun peeks over the mountain
and meets us in the city.

✳

Even in the early morning,
Port-au-Prince is crowded
with people.
Stay close, Papa says,
squeezing my hand.

Papa! I'm not a baby!
I remind him.

All around us,
the city teems with sights,
smells, and sounds.

Baskets are piled high
with brightly colored fruit—
green and yellow bananas,
grapefruit and mangoes,
lemons and limes.

In an open pot, hot oil sizzles.
Fried plantains and sweet potatoes
crackle and sputter.
Chicken wings hiss and frizzle
in wide silver frying pans.

Tap-taps rumble and honk.
Old cars rattle and cough.
Welcome to the city, Serafina!
they seem to say.

I love it here! I shout back.

We pass the clean white palace
where the president lives.

A long iron fence surrounds
thick green grass
and winding stone paths.

I wonder how lush grass
and smooth stones
feel under bare feet.
How pleasant it would be
if the path to the ravine
were as soft and lovely
as the path around
the President's Palace.
I curl my toes
and try to ignore
the scratching bark
and prickly straw.

Outside the fence,
people sing and wave
small blue-and-red flags.

Inside the fence,
above rows of windows
and mighty chalk columns,
a large flag floats proudly.

Blue for hope.
Red for blood.

Not just slave blood,
my blood,
the blood of my granpè.

Watch over me, Granpè,
I pray.
Please bring back my courage
so I can talk to Papa.
Help him to understand
the way you would.

✳
✳

The parade isn't until
late afternoon,
but already drums beat,
maracas rattle and swish.
Men in straw hats
and brightly colored shirts
blow and tap their
painted bamboo trumpets.

I squeeze Papa's hand.
I like to be alone with him,
but still,
I wish Manman and Gogo
didn't have clothes to wash.
I wish they didn't have
mint and thyme to bundle.

I close my eyes and gather
the music and colors
in my arms,
a holiday bouquet
to bring back
to Manman and Gogo.
Sometimes happiness
eases hunger
better than rice and beans.

When I open my eyes again,
a woman holds out
a stalk of sugarcane.
Papa shakes his head

and frowns.
I know we have no money
for treats,
but I don't care.
We're in the city!

Papa twirls me past
the big white church
where we pray on Sunday.
Past small shops
with green awnings,
and pink apartments
with clothes hanging
from the railings.

When we pass the blue cafe
with the rainbow umbrellas,
I know we are almost at
Papa's supermarket.

✳
* ✳
*

Papa's supermarket is the biggest,
busiest market in Port-au-Prince.
Remember, Serafina, he says,
as we step inside,
you must be quiet and let me work.

I know, Papa! I say. *I know!*
I sit on a wooden crate
and watch Papa pour
sacks and sacks of Miami rice
into brown barrels.

Gogo says that Haiti rice tastes better
than Miami rice.
Gogo says that Haiti rice is healthier
than Miami rice.

Papa says that nobody buys
Haiti rice anymore.
Why should they?
Miami rice costs less money.

Cheap is not better,
Gogo always says,
shrugging her shoulders.
But an empty sack cannot stand.

In the barrels, the rice sparkles
like tiny white stars.
I say the best rice
is the rice that fills our bellies.

*

When Papa goes
to find his boss,
Mr. Pétion,
I watch a caterpillar
in a heavy yellow coat
climb up the rice barrel.
I pick it up.
It slithers and slumps
across my fingers
and up my arm.

*Do you know what you'll be
when you grow up?* I ask.
Before I can tell her,
Papa comes back.

Swiv mwen, he says, *follow me.
Mr. Pétion is having
a Flag Day celebration
at his house.
He asked me to deliver
a crate of black mushrooms
and a tank of lobsters.
The wagon is already packed.*

I follow Papa outside
to the front of the store
and place my caterpillar
on a scraggly weed
poking through the cement.
Good luck! I whisper.

Papa grabs the handle
of a large red wagon
and we begin walking.

Inside the tank,
a huddle of lobsters
with rubber-banded claws
peer at me.
I wave to them.
The lobsters are alive! I say.

Papa laughs.
For a little while . . .
but don't get too attached!

* ✳
*
*

Mr. Pétion's house sits high on the hill.
A tall girl, skinnier than a spider's leg,
opens the door for us.
I smile, but she just nods
and motions for us
to follow her inside.

Mr. Pétion's house is cold
like the refrigerator
in the back of Papa's store.
It has an inside stove
and a long table
with wooden chairs.

On the roof,
there's a pool of water
to swim in
and even a house
for Mr. Pétion's car!

When I'm a doctor,
I'll have a car too.
I'll visit old people
who live far from the city.
I'll take sick babies
to the hospital to get better.

But I'll never build
a house for my car.
People need houses
more than cars do.

✳
＊ ＊
＊

Papa empties the wagon
and parks it outside the car house.
Trumpets and drums
bellow in the distance.

Bom-bom
Bom-bom
Bom-bom

We're going to miss the parade!
I say.

Papa laughs. *No we won't!*
He grabs my hand
and swings my arm.
Walking downhill is like flying!

At last we're back
in the heat of the city.
The closer and louder
the trumpets and drums,
the more crowded
the busy streets become.

Bom-bom
Bom-bom
Bom-bom

Soon the drums
beat inside of me
like my own heart.

✳

Bom-bom
Bom-bom
Bom-bom

A group of grown-up dancers
dressed in white
carry flags of blue and red.
They step and bounce,
step and clap.
They shake their shoulders
and sway their hips.

The drums beat
without stopping,
steady like a heart.

Bom-bom
Bom-bom
Bom-bom

I'd like to step and sway
in a flowing dress
and shake my shoulders free.
I'd like to clap my hands
and stamp my feet,
moving to nothing
but the beat of a drum.

✳

Next, children my age
dressed in yellow uniforms
with socks inside their shiny shoes
march to the center of the street.

Look! Papa says, *There's Nadia!*
Nadia waves, but
without even thinking,
I pretend I don't see.

The drums beat
without stopping.

Bom-bom
Bom-bom
Bom-bom

Nadia and her school friends
hold hands and form a circle.
They sing a song of freedom.

Let there be no traitors in our ranks.
Let us be masters of our soil.

I think about the Tonton Macoutes.
The Tonton Macoutes were traitors.
I'm glad they are gone.

I wish Granpè were still here,
but now I'm beginning
to understand.

Granpè only wanted to be
master of his soil.
My heart beats
in steady rhythm
with the drums.

Bom-bom
Bom-bom
Bom-bom

For the rest of the parade,
I feel Granpè's heart
beat inside of mine.

＊

Colors, sounds, and smells
float through my mind
as Papa and I walk home
in happy silence.

When I see a heart-shaped rock
lying in the road,
I let go of Papa's hand,
pick it up, and squeeze it
in my fist.
I say a silent prayer to Granpè
for courage,
then take a deep breath.

Papa, I say,
I know Manman needs me.
I know it's important
to do my chores.

Papa listens quietly.
He doesn't interrupt
like Manman would.

I want to be a doctor, Papa.
And to be a doctor,
I must go to school.
Gogo told me that Granpè
could read.
He wanted to teach Manman
to read too.
Did you know that Granpè said

education is the road to freedom?

Papa doesn't say anything
so I keep talking.

*I think it would make Granpè happy
for me to go to school and become a doctor.
You said yourself that I have a gift.*

Papa is still quiet
so I go on.

*If I become a doctor,
I can help Manman even more.
One day, I'll earn enough money
to buy chicken and pork.
Manman and Gogo
won't have to work so hard.
And, Papa, when I'm a doctor,
I'll have my own car.
You won't have to walk so far to work
or pull a wagon up the hill to your boss's house.
Please, Papa, please think about it.
I want to go to school
more than anything in the world.*

I stop talking, hold my breath,
and squeeze
my heart-shaped rock.

For a little while, all I hear
is the soft brushing of feet
through grass
and my own heart beating
in my chest.

Bom-bom
Bom-bom
Bom-bom

Finally Papa stops walking
and looks at me.
Well, Serafina, he says,
I can tell you've thought about this.

The scent of mangoes, oranges,
and wild thyme surrounds us.

Papa puts his hands on my shoulders.
You must understand
books and a uniform cost
more money than we have.

My heart slows and sinks.
Silence hangs over us
like an overripe mango,
dotted with worms
and maggots.
I stare at the ground
and bite my lip
to keep from crying.

Papa takes my face in his hands.
He lifts my chin so our eyes meet.
But maybe, maybe there is a way.
I can hear that this is important to you.

The warmth of Papa's hands and voice
raise my sinking heart.
Hope flutters in my chest.

Papa's eyes are soft but steady.
You would have to help earn money
for books and a uniform.
The new school year
starts in September.
That gives you a little more
than three months.

My heart leaps.
Really?
Mèsi! Thank you!
I can wait!
I can earn money!
Mèsi! Mèsi! I say,
jumping up
and walking backward.

Papa smiles.
Then his face turns serious.
There is one more thing.

What, Papa? I ask.
I'll do anything!

You must clear all of this
with Manman first.

Hope drains away
like water in a cracked basin.

But, Papa,
Manman will never agree.
All she thinks about is work,
and she worries about everything.
You're the only one
who can convince her.

Papa shakes his head.
I have faith in you, Serafina.
If this is important enough,
you'll help her to understand.

✳

I push away thoughts
of Manman and her worries.
The whole way home,
my mind bursts with ideas
for how to earn money.

If I start my chores earlier,
I can help Manman and Gogo
gather and bundle more herbs
to sell in the city.

And I have another idea too.

*Papa, did you know
Gogo and Granpè had a garden?
They even had chickens!
I'll ask Gogo to help me
start a vegetable garden.
We can grow our own food to sell
so we can save for books and a uniform.
Maybe we can even keep a few chickens!*

Maybe, Papa says, grinning.

By the time we reach home,
ideas tumble and bounce
in my brain faster
than spring rain.

The only problem
is how to tell Manman.

✳

The smell of garlic and smoke
floating toward us
reminds me of how hungry I am.

Manman stands by the cooking fire
stirring rice and beans.
Gogo sits in the doorway
tying little bundles of thyme.

Manman! I cry.

I rush into her arms
with my holiday bouquet
of music, color,
and all the happiness
that hope brings.

Serafina, the fire! Be careful!
Manman's voice is sharp
as the sugarcane leaf.

I step away from the fire.

Manman nods at the bucket
by the door.
There's only a little water left.
Better wash up, she says.

The music and color
begin to fade,
but I won't let them.

I'll be so patient and good,
Manman will have to say yes.

Here, I say,
reaching into my pocket
and handing Manman
the heart-shaped rock.

O*h, Serafina!* she says.
Mèsi anpil. Thank you so much.
Her voice is warm and gentle now.

After dinner, I'll get more water,
I say cheerfully,
hoping to keep Manman happy.

✳

That night, before we sleep,
Gogo tells me that
she's proud of me.

Even after your long day,
you were extra helpful
to your manman.

I try to think of something
to say, but Gogo doesn't wait
for a response.

Your manman works hard.
She tries her best, but she's tired.
Her mind and heart
are full of worry.

We're both quiet.

Manman's worries
are like the mosquitoes
at the ravine, so many
you could never count them
or get rid of them all.

Even if I am patient and good,
will I be able to convince her
to let me go to school?

In my mind, I see Manman
stirring dry rice,

picking out tiny speck-like bugs,
and flicking them to the ground.
I hear her humming contentedly
while she works.
How can that make her happy?

When I grow up,
I want to do
more important things
than pluck bugs from rice.

How can I make
Manman understand?

Gogo? I whisper.
Are you sleeping?

Not yet, Serafina,
she says,
but her voice
is low and drowsy.
Tell me again
about the dancers.

The day after Flag Day
is cloudy and dark.
I don't like the rainy season
but Gogo always says,
*Remember the rain
that grew your corn.*
When I remind her
that we don't have corn,
she just laughs.

Julie Marie is washing clothes
at the ravine when I get there.
She greets me with a large,
sparkling smile.
I remember what Papa said
about her father struggling
to feed his family.
I wish I'd saved her
something to eat.

Tell me everything,
Julie Marie says.
Did you see the parade?
Did you ask your papa about school?
I thought about you all day.
Tell me everything!

I describe the lobsters
and the house
for Mr. Pétion's car.
I tell her about the music

and the dancers.
I saw Nadia too! I say.
I don't tell her
that I didn't wave.

And school?
Did you ask your papa
about school?

I tell her everything
that Papa said
and all my ideas
to save money.
But I'm afraid
Manman won't understand.

Julie Marie flashes
her sparkling smile.
She will.
Mothers only want
what's best.

✳

Maybe Julie Marie is right.
Maybe I am misjudging Manman.

I hurry home and quickly
sweep the floor,
gather the wood,
and pile the charcoal.

When I see Manman and Gogo
coming down the path,
I run to meet them.

Serafina! Is everything okay?
Manman asks.

Wi, wi, I say, *but I need
to ask you something important.*

Did you finish your chores?

I nod. *Please, Manman,
it's very important.*
I hold the curtain open
so Manman and Gogo
can place their baskets
on the freshly swept dirt floor.

*You help your mother
bundle the herbs,* Gogo says.
I'll go outside and start dinner.

Manman pulls out
tiny sprigs of thyme
and spreads them
on the table.
What's so important, Serafina?
she asks.

I clear my throat
and take a deep breath.

✳

Manman, I would like
to go to school,
I say steadily.
And then, without stopping
to breathe
or to let her interrupt,
I tell her everything—
about wanting to be a doctor
like Antoinette Solaine
and what Papa said
about helping to save money
for books and a uniform.
I promise her that I will still
get all my chores done.
I am old enough to do more
than gather wood and water.
This is my dream, Manman.
I want this more than
anything in the world.

Before I even finish my last sentence,
Manman shakes her head.
School? Serafina, we have
a new baby coming!
If you want more grown-up chores,
Gogo and I will take you
with us to the city.
You can wash the clothes
and help prepare
the rice and beans.

Suddenly I forget
all about being patient.

Manman! I don't want
to pick bugs out of rice!
I want to be a doctor!
I want to help save babies like Pierre.
And to be a doctor, I must go to school.
Don't you remember your own papa?
Granpè wanted you to read too!
If he were here, he would want me
to go to school and learn to read.
Don't you remember what he said?
Education is the path—

Manman interrupts, her voice
as fragile as a sparrow's egg.

—to freedom?
Were my father's books able to save him?
Be happy with what you have, Serafina.

I turn away,
my mind full of prickles and stings.

Manman can be happy
washing clothes
and sifting rice,
but I won't ever be!

At dinnertime,
Papa still wants to talk
about the parade.
He brings me a small flag
left over from his boss's party.

Mèsi, I say.
I bring my bowl of rice outside
and stick the flag in the dirt.
Papa sits on the ground
beside me.
Gogo stays inside with Manman.

We eat without talking,
but finally Papa asks
what happened.
Why are you so quiet?
Why is Manman so sad?

I shrug.
The words in my mind
still scratch and sting.
Papa keeps eating.
He doesn't push me to answer.

While we wash the dishes,
Gogo tries to talk,
but I'm not ready yet.

When we're done,
I get my stethoscope

and look for Banza.
Sometimes in the evening
I find him sniffing garbage
in the alley between
Julie Marie's house and Nadia's.
He always comes when I call
and lets me listen to his heart.
Sometimes Julie Marie plays with us.

But tonight,
there's no sign of Banza
or Julie Marie anywhere.
The alley is dark and empty
with the threat of rain.
The only one outside is me—
me and my sputtering bees.

✳

Hurry before the rain comes,
Gogo says the next morning.
She gives me the bucket
and pushes me out the door.
A sagging, shapeless sun
slumps purple, orange,
and heavy in the dark sky.

Why don't we just wait
for the rain? I ask.

Gogo shakes her head.
If you want your eggs hatched,
sit on them yourself! Now go!

I carry my bucket to the small stream
flowing down the other side of the alley.
It isn't a real stream, just a footpath
that gathers rainwater.
It's closer than the place
where we wash our clothes,
and take our baths,
where we gather water when
the rains don't come.

Manman's words buzz in my head.
Be happy with what you have.

What do we have? I wonder.
The bees in my brain grumble furiously.
Just work, work, work!

✳

The first drops are slow
and long in coming.

tumpa   tumpa   tumpa   tumpa

I scrape my bucket along
the bottom of the muddy stream.
Water bubbles and brims
over the narrow opening.

tumpa tumpa tumpa tumpa

The purple sky sags
low enough for me to touch.
Serafina, I hear Manman call.
Serafina! Hurry, Serafina!

Mud and water
squeeze between my toes.

tumpa tumpa tumpa tumpa

Mud and water
rush down the mountain
and suddenly swell
higher than my knee.

tumpatumpatumpatumpatumpatumpa

Purple folds into black.
Serafina! Gogo screams.

I drop my bucket
and drag my legs
through clinging mud
and rising water.

Manman and Gogo
rush toward me.
We clutch each other
and watch a blur
of dark gray rain
sweep across
the muddy alley.

A giant wet shadow
with shimmery arms
glides into our doorway,
lifts our house,

and carries it away.

I scream,
but Manman and Gogo
pull me along.

Arm in arm,
we wade against
the rising water.

Gogo carries a basket
of rice and beans on her head.
Without stopping,
Manman lifts me onto her back.

Manman, I whisper.
I'm too heavy for you!

Shhhh . . . hold on tight.

My fingers clutch
the yellow tail of her scarf.
I bury my head
in her soaked shoulder.

Broken branches, spoons,
and empty pots drift by.
Close your eyes, Manman says
when the dead donkey floats down.

I close my eyes

but still I see.

*
* *
*

On and on we wade.
Water swells to the hem
of my dress.

Manman! I cry.
Are you sure
I'm not too heavy?

Shhhh, Manman says again.

At every step,
the water rises.
I look behind us.

Nadia's mother struggles,
a bag of rice and a baby in her arms.

Manman! I whisper,
Nadia's mother—

The sounds of rain
and rushing water,
of children screaming
and mothers crying,
swallow my words.

When I look back again,
Nadia's mother is gone.

What happened?
Where did she go?

✳
*   *
*

Manman's shoulders heave
and I wrap my arms
tighter around her.
A man in a pink shirt
offers to carry me.
Manman shakes her head
and shifts me higher on her back.
Gogo's arm pulls us to one side,
but we keep going.

Where are Julie Marie and Nadia?
Where are their brothers and sisters?
Are they safe?

Hail Mary, full of grace,
Manman begins to pray.
Her shoulders shake so hard,
I'm afraid I'll fall
into the water and disappear.

Mwen pè, I whisper
close to Manman's ears.
I'm scared.

Manman's shoulders still shake
but her voice is strong.
Ou dwe brav, Serafina, be brave.

Manman worries about everything.
How can she be so brave?

The rain stops.

The muddy water drops
lower than Manman's knee.

I can walk now, Manman,
I say.

Manman doesn't answer
or put me down.

My arms tingle and twitch.
Manman, I can walk now.

Shhh . . . Serafina.
Look for Papa.

Slowly we slog
through the sinking city.

Papa will be waiting
at our meeting place,
outside the President's Palace.

Papa will make everything
all right.

PART

TWO

Marie Rose! Serafina!
Gogo!

Papa's hearty voice
skims the water.
He sloshes toward us,
and lifts me in his arms.

Papa! The rain washed away
our house!

Manman whimpers
like a lost and hungry kitten,
but Gogo stays quiet
as the moon.

I bury my head in Papa's
wide, sturdy shoulders
and cry.

You're safe. Bondye bon,
Papa says and hugs us all
for a long time.
We can build another home.
The important thing
is that we're together.
You're safe.

We follow a swampy
new path out of the city.

Water remains thick
around Papa's ankles,
but already the sun
has baked our clothes dry.
Every few minutes
Manman squeaks softly.
Papa reaches for her hand.
Mwen regrèt, he says.

Why is Papa sorry?
It's not his fault
the rains came.

✳

Walking close together,
we climb a mountain
I have never seen before.
The path is long and steep
and far from home.
Tiny, pretty colored shacks
dot the hillside,
but there are no pink flowers
or wild thyme.

We climb and climb
until we find a wide-open space
far away from other houses.
That night we sleep
on leaf-covered stones.
We wait for the earth to dry
and try to ignore
the grumble in our stomachs.

I wonder about my friends.
Did Nadia find her mother?
Where is Julie Marie?
What happened to Banza?
I listen to the crickets
and tree frogs,
and to Papa's broken voice
comforting Manman.

Look, he whispers,
the stars still shine.

Gogo squeezes my hand.
I have a surprise, she says.
In the silvery hilltop darkness,
she hands me my doctor bell.

It twinkles
like a misplaced star.

✳
 ✳

The next day, Gogo explores.
Manman and I sift
through roots and rocks
to clear a space for our new house.
While we work,
I worry about my friends.
Where are they?
I worry about Banza
and Baby Pierre.
Who will visit his little grave
and talk to him?

Manman tries to cheer me.
*Did you know my papa liked
to sing?* she asks. *Just like your papa!
Together we would shake dry gourds
and march through our garden,
waking up the sleeping seeds
with our silly songs.*
Manman touches my face.
Her fingers smell of dirt and roots.
*Life is hard, Serafina, but we always
work and hope for something better.*
She reaches into her pocket,
then wraps my fingers
around the small heart-shaped rock
that I gave her on Flag Day.
*I love you, Serafina,
and nothing is stronger than love.
No matter what happens,
we beat the drum and we dance again.*

✳

After work, Papa lugs home
a striped bedsheet
filled with slabs of wood,
crumpled tin,
and scraps from other people's
deserted houses.

It takes Papa longer
to walk to the city now,
but he doesn't complain.
There's more space here, he says.
He smiles at Manman.
We'll build a new house,
a stronger house.
Then he looks at Gogo and me.
He empties his pocket
and shows us tiny packages
of paper-wrapped seeds.
We even have room for a garden, he says.
We'll plant basil and thyme,
horsemint, hot peppers,
amaranth, and tomatoes.

He gives Gogo the seeds,
reaches for my hand,
and twirls me through the grass.

For the first time in two days,
I feel a smile on my face.

Oh, how I love my papa!

*
* *
*

First we need to clear a spot,
Gogo says the very next morning.

After I gather water and wood,
I help Gogo remove rocks,
twigs, and broken branches
from a sunny space
beside the place
where Papa will build our house.

Gogo shows me how to plant seeds.
Not too close, not too deep.
Give your seeds space to sleep.

Clearing the land is hard work,
but I've never seen Gogo so happy.
We'll need extra water for our seeds,
she says.

As I carry my bucket
down the long, winding gully
that leads to the ravine,
I wonder again
where my friends were
when the rains came.
Where are Julie Marie and Nadia now?
What happened to Nadia's mother?
Who'll take care of Nadia
if her mother is gone?
Who would take care of me
if something happened to Manman?

Papa could lift me above the flood,
and Gogo could tell me stories,
but who would make sure I ate enough,
and remind me to wash my hands
after I played with Banza?
Who would clean my clothes
and let me listen to her broken heart?

Even an empty bucket feels heavy
when I think of losing Manman.

*
 * *
  *

I try to cheer myself
with thoughts of tiny seeds
snuggled in the ground,
waiting to grow.
But all my thoughts
lead back to my lost friends.

Church is just three days away.
I hope when Sunday comes,
we'll all be together again.

My other hopes—
of going to school
and becoming a doctor
with Julie Marie—
feel like faraway dreams
belonging to somebody else.

       ✳
   ✳   ✳
       ✳

On Saturday, Manman and Gogo
walk with Papa into the city.
Papa has given them a few coins
to buy new clothes
from the used clothes
piled on every corner.

Manman asks me
to come along.

I have never passed up
a trip to the city,
but now the walk is long.
My heart and bones
are heavy as cinder blocks.

I shake my head.

Manman studies me,
worry in her eyes.
Ser—

I'm okay, I tell her. *Just tired.*

Manman strokes my cheek.
We won't be too long.
I promise.

✳

As I pull the tiny weeds
that popped up overnight,
my friends drift into my mind.

Why didn't I wave to Nadia
at the parade?

What would Julie Marie say
if she knew
my dream of becoming a doctor
had floated away?

What about Banza?
Where is he?
In my mind, I see him
wandering alone and hungry,
with no one to sneak him food
or pull the prickles from his paws.

Will I ever see any of them again?

Before I know it,
the burrs and brambles
that twist around my heart
break apart,
and I choke on a flood of tears.

✳
* ✳
*

For a long time,
I sit in the garden
and let myself cry.
It feels strange
to be so alone,
with no one
to cheer me
with riddles or songs,
or sloppy dog kisses.

Every time I think I'm empty,
the tears swell and burst again.
I rub my eyes and my nose,
take a deep breath,
and stand up.
Manman and Gogo
will be home soon.
There's work to do.

The water bucket
is propped against our stack of wood.
Papa says it will be weeks
before he has enough boards
to begin to build our house.
I miss the comfort of walls
and a roof,
the cozy shelter
of being inside.

When I get to the ravine,
I dip the bucket

deep, deep down
and watch the water
bubble and flow.

My thoughts are so far away
that I don't even greet the girl
kneeling by the water's edge,
scrubbing clothes.

A seabird flies overhead.

The girl looks up.
Tiny braids spiral down
her forehead.
Her dark eyes are as shiny
as the seeds of the sapote fruit.

Julie Marie?!
I shout.

She drops the shirt she's washing.

Serafina?!

I drop my bucket.
We race into each other's arms,
hugging and squeezing
so tight we can't breathe.

Finally questions tumble out:
Did your house get washed away too?

What happened to Nadia?
The roof blew off and the walls caved in!
I saw her mother disappear—
We're all safe—
My family too.

Julie Marie looks at the clothes
at her feet.
These are all we have left.
But we're safe! She says.
And we found each other!

✳

Small shirts, large shirts,
small shorts, large shorts,
flowered skirts,
and brightly colored dresses.

I help Julie Marie pound and rub,
dip and rinse, until our fingers
are tiny wrinkled twigs.

Suddenly I love doing chores!

Uncle Bouki, Uncle Bouki,
Julie Marie sings.
We hang wet clothes
on spiny bushes and scrubby trees.

For the first time
since the rains came,
I sing too.
Are you sleeping? Are you sleeping?

After all the clothes are hung,
Julie Marie and I talk.
I tell her how Manman
doesn't want me to go to school.
How I should be happy
with what I have.
I think Manman is right.
I should just stay home
and help her and Gogo.

Julie Marie's eyes widen
in disbelief.
I look down at my bare feet.
The flood washed away
my courage,
I say quietly.

But, Serafina, the flood is over.
Don't let it destroy our dream.
Without dreams the world
is only dirt and dust.

I study Julie Marie's bright face.

How can she have so much faith
when her family struggles every day,
when she might never
have enough money
for books and a uniform?

Her hope wakes mine
from its sleep.
I'll think about it, I say.

Julie Marie smiles.
Bon! Thinking leads to dreaming!

＊
＊　＊
＊

We head home.
Julie Marie walks one way.
I walk the other.
When I see Manman and Gogo
climbing the hill,
I race to meet them.
Words tumble
out of my mouth.

I found Julie Marie!
Her family settled not far from us.
I was getting water
and she was washing clothes!
Just like at home!

Bondye bon! Gogo says.

Manman puts down
her silver tub.
She hugs me,
smoothes the hair
from my face,
and kisses me.

I'm so happy for you, Serafina!
I'm so happy for you both.
Now come with me.
I have a surprise for you.

✳

Together we walk
back to the ravine.
Manman spreads new clothes
on a large rock.
For Papa,
two shirts and a pair of shorts.
For Manman,
a bright blue blouse and a skirt
decorated with small yellow stars.
For Gogo,
a brown dress large enough
to make two dresses.
Finally Manman unrolls
a shiny green dress.
Tiny pink stitches
stretch across the top.
Tiny pink flowers
dance along the bottom.

For me? I ask.
Manman smiles and nods.
I take the dress in my arms and twirl.

We soak the clothes in watery vinegar
and pound them with a heavy stick.

To banish bad spirits, Manman says.

How could bad spirits
hide in such a beautiful dress?

In the morning,
I put on my new dress
and we parade to church.
I link arms with Julie Marie.
Behind us, the grown-ups
talk quietly.

I hope we see Nadia, I say.
Then I remember the parade,
and sagging regret spoils
my new-dress feeling.

When we finally reach the church,
my legs are as weak and floppy
as a papaya stem.

The priest kisses the altar
and sings, *Bondye bon!*

Bondye bon! we all sing.
We raise our arms
and clap our hands.
Bondye bon! God is good!

God is good,
but still people disappeared
in the flood.
Still people died.
The priest reads off a
list of names.
He tells us about each one.

An old man who carved birds
from pieces of wood.
A woman who took care
of orphaned children.
Nadia's mother.

Julie Marie squeezes my hand.
I feel a tear roll down my cheek.

Other people have relocated,
the priest says.
We are not sure where.

On the way home,
we talk quietly
like grown-ups.

*I wonder if we'll ever
see Nadia again,*
Julie Marie says.

I hope so, I say
and wish I had waved
when I had the chance.

✳

Papa brings home more seeds—
beans, sweet potatoes,
spinach, and peppermint.
Gogo and I clear more land.

Now I gather water
four times a day.
Twice for Manman
and twice for our garden.

At night, Gogo tells me
about each plant.
If you burn two basil leaves
on a piece of charcoal,
she says,
you'll know if you'll have
a happy marriage.
Leaves that sputter and snap
mean trouble.
Leaves that burn quietly
promise happiness.

Did you burn basil leaves
when you met Granpè?
I ask.

Gogo's voice is sad.
The leaves burned slowly,
but not long enough.

*

In one corner of the garden
there's a patch of rocky soil.
Gogo says nothing will grow there.

Let me try, I beg.
Gogo smiles and hands me
peppermint seeds to plant.

I water them
and say a little prayer.
I weed around them
and make a little promise.

If you grow leaves, little seeds,
we'll dress you in ribbons
and bring you to the city!

Gogo laughs, but in time,
I know my happy little seeds
will grow!

✳

After work,
every day for weeks
and weeks and weeks,
we clear away
fallen branches
and small rocks.

June melts into July
and July into August.
Papa drags up
more slats
of rotting wood
and more sheets
of discarded tin.
He brings home
more bent nails
and rusty bolts.

Manman's belly is wider
than a watermelon,
but still she helps us
measure and hold,
lift and hammer.
Julie Marie's papa helps too.

When at last
our new house is done,
Manman washes
the striped sheet
and hangs it up,

changing one room
into two.

Straw on the floor
for Gogo and me.
Straw on the floor
for Papa, Manman,
and the new baby
when it comes.

Gogo says babies
are a blessing from God.

Every night I pray
this baby will live
and bless my family.

✳
∗ ∗
∗

The day after the house
is finished,
Manman is too tired
to go with Gogo to the city
to sell our basil and mint.

I wish I could go instead,
but Gogo says I must stay
and finish my chores.

Tim tim, Julie Marie calls
from outside our door.
She carefully balances
a basket of dirty laundry
on her head. .

Bwa sèch, I answer.
I find my water bucket
and together we walk
to the ravine.

*What stands on four feet
but cannot run?*

That's easy, I say. *A chair!*

Julie Marie laughs
and shakes her head.
Non! A table.

I fill my bucket
and wait for Julie Marie
to finish washing.
We hang wet clothes
and collect firewood.
When Julie Marie's basket
brims with dry branches,
I balance the bucket on my head
and we walk home.

School starts next month, Julie Marie says.
Have you thought about
talking to your manman again?

Not really, but maybe I should.
Our baby will be here soon
and the coin jar is starting to fill
with garden coins.
Papa says Mr. Pétion might even buy
some of our vegetables!
Julie Marie smiles,
and I remember all the plans
we had before the flood—
to both go to school,
to both become doctors,
and to one day open a clinic together.

I remember the promise
I made to myself and to Granpè.
Something stirs inside my heart.
My faraway dreams are floating back!

✳

When I get home,
Manman is on her bed,
groaning.

Serafina! she says.
Her face glistens
with tiny beads of sweat.
Prese! Hurry!
Get Julie Marie's mother.

Manman! Are you sick?

Prese! The baby is coming!

What about the midwife?

There's no time, Serafina!
Prese!

I run down the path that leads
to Julie Marie's house.
Julie Marie's mother is outside,
a baby in one arm,
a wooden spoon in the other.

Prese! Prese! Gogo is in the city
and our baby is coming!

Julie Marie comes outside
carrying her brother Michel.
She sits him in the dirt
and takes the baby
and the wooden spoon.

Her mother hurries inside her house
and brings out a handful
of rags and the top of an old tin can.
Prese! Prese! she says. *Let's go!*

As we hurry down the hill,
Julie Marie calls after me,
You'll be a wonderful big sister!

*

By the time we get back,
Manman is holding a small,
wrinkled baby.
Come see your brother Gregory,
she says weakly.

I kneel beside her.
What can I do to help you,
Manman? I whisper.

Julie Marie's mother gives me
a soft, clean cloth.
Bondye bon, Marie Rose,
your son is beautiful.

A long, slippery cord stretches
from Gregory to Manman.
While I gently wipe
Manman's face,
Julie Marie's mother
cuts the cord
with the top of the tin can.
Then she takes Gregory
and wraps him
in a clean blanket.
Hold your brother
while I sweep and freshen
your mother's bed,
she says, shooing me outside.

I sit on a large rock.

Hello, Gregory, I whisper.
I hold his face
close to mine.
His eyes are closed
like a baby kitten's,
and he has a musty smell,
like the leftover scent
in Gogo's basket of herbs.

Gogo says you're a blessing.
Please bless our family.

Gregory's tininess
tugs at my heart.
I think about Baby Pierre.
I promise, Gregory,
I'll do my best
to make sure
Manman eats.
I promise to do
everything I can
to keep you safe.

✳

The next day,
Papa brings home
two sweet potatoes
for us to fry.

Gogo makes Manman
tizann, a special
healing herbal tea.
Manman smiles happily
at Gregory's round,
wrinkled face.

Papa turns the washtub over
and beats out a happy song.

The sun rises,
the sun sets,
little by little the bird
builds its nest!

Gogo takes my hand.
We sway our hips
and flutter our arms
like parade dancers.

Gregory is a blessing!
My heart floats,
and my belly is stuffed
with sweet fried joy!

When Manman washes up
in the mornings,
I hold Gregory
and sing him songs.
Manman and Gogo tell me
how helpful I am,
what a good big sister.

Day by day,
Manman grows stronger
and happier.
Gregory's tummy
is quickly becoming round
as the mango.

✳

After I help Manman with Gregory,
I meet Julie Marie at the ravine.
Sometimes I wash clothes too.
While we work, we talk about Nadia
and say prayers for her and her family.
We talk about our clinic
and try to decide what to call it.

In the afternoons,
when Julie Marie finishes her chores,
she helps me in the garden.
She can't come every day,
but when she does,
the afternoon passes quickly.

We pick and bundle the best herbs
and vegetables,
some for Manman and Gogo
to sell in the city,
some for Papa to bring to Mr. Pétion.
Julie Marie helps me clear away
the pebbles and weeds that could choke
my fragile peppermint plants.

As soon as they grow,
I'm going to bundle them in ribbons
so Manman can bring them to the city too,
I tell Julie Marie.

She grins.
More coins for the uniform jar!

The lima beans
are still tiny sprouts,
but the amaranth
is higher than my knee.

Gogo smiles.
You're like the amaranth—
beautiful and strong,
sheltering the smaller buds,
coaxing them to grow.

Gogo's words make me feel taller.
People really are like plants—
kind words make them grow.

Later, while Gogo bundles herbs
to sweeten Manman's bathwater,
I care for Gregory.

Little brother, little brother, I sing.
Do you know? Do you know?
Your big sister loves you.
Your big sister loves you.
Bom. Bom. Bom. Bom. Bom. Bom.

Gogo says Gregory
is too young
to smile,
but I know
he's smiling at me.

*
*
*

One afternoon, I see
tiny peppermint leaves
poking through the rocks.
As soon as Julie Marie arrives,
I show her.
Gogo said pushing
through the dry earth
is the hardest part.
Now our peppermint
will stretch in the sun!
When Manman sees
how hard I've been working,
I know she'll let me
go to school.
I grab Julie Marie's hand.
We're going to be doctors!

Julie Marie smiles,
but her smile
pulls tight on her face.

What is it? I ask.

I can never go to school, Serafina.

Did you talk to your papa?

Julie Marie shakes her head.

Then how do you know he'll say no?

A fat tear rolls down
Julie Marie's cheek.
My papa has too many
hungry mouths to feed.

But you said—

I know, Serafina.
I didn't want you
to give up.
You should be a doctor
even if I can't.

We are both quiet a long while.

Mwen regrèt sa, I finally say.
I promise I'll teach you
everything I learn.
Maybe I can grow
enough peppermint
for two uniforms!

✳
✳
✳

I spend every free moment
in the garden,
weeding, watering,
and watching
my peppermint plants
grow taller!

One day, when Gogo,
Manman, and Gregory
are in the city,
I hear a loud rustle
in the bushes.

Who's there? I yell loudly,
hoping to scare away
a wild pig or rat.
Ale lwen! Go away!
This is my garden!

I stand up, and giant
ginger-colored paws
almost knock me down!

Banza! I scream.

Banza yelps
and runs in circles.

Banza! You found me!

I haven't any food to give him,
but still his tail wags furiously
and he licks my face.

Let me see those paws!
Any prickles?

I try to grab his leg,
but he runs away.
Don't forget, I call after him.
This is our new home!

Nobody can believe
that Banza found his way
up and around so many hills.
Not Manman or Gogo,
Papa or Julie Marie.
Nobody can believe
he found me.

It shows how much
kindness and love matter!
Papa says.
Love always finds a way.
The important thing
is to never give up.

✳

It's hard to imagine that
just a few months ago,
all I could think about was rain,
and rebuilding,
and Manman's worries.

Now the rainy season is long past.
Our new house is warm, sturdy, and dry.
Gregory is growing healthy and strong.

At night, I listen
to Manman and Papa talk quietly.
Sometimes Manman's rippling laugh
mixes with Papa's cheerful rumble.
Sometimes I hear her sing quietly
to Gregory and I wonder
if they are the same songs
she sang with Granpè.

Papa said
everything would be better
when the baby came.
And it is.

Julie Marie said,
Without dreams the world
is only dirt and dust.

School starts in less than two weeks.
It's time to talk to Manman again.

*
  *
 *

Before I talk to Manman,
I'll talk to Papa.
Maybe he's changed his mind.
Maybe this time he'll agree
to talk to Manman for me.

Manman, I say
while she nurses Gregory
before supper.
*May I go down the hill
to meet Papa?*

Wi! Manman says,
smiling at me.
*Just don't walk too far—
only to the bottom of the hill.*

*Mèsi! I'll hide
behind a banana tree.
Papa will be so surprised!*

I hurry to the bottom
of the hill
and sit beneath
a large banana tree.
When I see Papa,
I run into his arms.
He lifts and twirls me.
*Serafina! What are you doing here?
Is everyone okay?*

Wi, Papa!
I just need to talk
to you alone.

Papa laughs.
What is it today,
my sweet Serafina?

You'll see! I take his hand.
Together we walk
up our last hill.
I pull him into the garden
and make him close his eyes.

Okay! Open them!

Amazing! Papa says
when he sees
the sturdy shoots
and bright green leaves.
Gogo didn't think anything
would grow in this soil.

Papa, I say,
our coin jar is filling fast.
Soon, some of the coins will be
peppermint coins.

Papa smiles.
He knows what
I'm trying to say.

I'm proud of you, Serafina.

The pride in his voice
gives me courage.

I pluck a peppermint leaf
and rub it between my fingers.

School starts very soon.
I still want to go.

Papa nods and takes my hand.
You've done everything
I've asked.
But there's one last step.

Papa, do you think
you could—

Papa shakes his head.
Serafina, Manman needs to hear
your voice,
your words,
your hope.

He squeezes my hand.
Now that Gregory is here,
she'll be able to listen better.

✳

After supper that night,
I walk to the ravine.
It's quiet.
Soft, shimmering light
wraps around me
like a golden cloak.

Manman seemed so
happy nursing Gregory
while Gogo and I
washed the dishes.

Maybe now is the right moment.

I watch the dark, warm water
flow into my bucket,
and think about Granpè.
I wish I could have known him.
Are you watching over me, Granpè?
Please help Manman to understand,
I whisper.

I think about Pierre.
I still miss him.
I don't need a cross made of stones
to remember you, Pierre.
Please help Manman to understand,
I beg.

I think about Gregory.
You're my special blessing,

baby brother.
Please help Manman to understand,
I pray.

The gentle amber light
softens to gray.
Crickets and tree frogs
begin their evening serenade.

I lift my bucket
and head up the hill.
Before I reach home,
I promise God
that if Manman lets me
go to school,
I will study hard
and never complain
about anything.

It's almost dark when I get home.
Papa, Manman, Gogo, and Gregory
are gathered in the garden.
By the light of the moon,
I see that Papa is smiling.
Gogo shakes the jar of coins
and swings her hips.
Manman holds Gregory
in one arm
and reaches out for me
with the other.
I put down the water bucket.

Whispered promises mingle
with the bold scent
of peppermint and thyme.
Manman, I say, looking into her
open, loving face.
*I want to talk to you
about school.*

Then, all in one breath,
I repeat everything
I said to Papa.
This time, Manman
doesn't interrupt.
She looks at the garden
and then at me.

*I see how hard you've been working.
The vegetables and herbs*

are thriving—even the peppermint!
Manman smiles.
You're becoming a strong,
dependable young woman.

I feel myself stretching
all the way to the moon.
Thank you, Manman.

Gogo thinks the jar
should be full in a week.

My heart is thumping.

Manman pauses
and holds my gaze.
And when the jar is full,
you may go to school.

Really, Manman?

Manman nods and laughs.
Really!

I jump and kiss them all.
I twirl my pretty green dress.
Mèsi! Mèsi! I shout.
I'm going to school!

✳

I can't wait to tell Julie Marie.
One more week
and the jar should be full.

Then I'm going to school!
Manman said it herself!
When the jar is full,
I'm going to school!

✱

The next day, I'm up early
to gather water
before I work in the garden.

Julie Marie is already
at the ravine.

I run down the hill to share
my good news,
but she has news
of her own.

Her words bubble out
like an overfilled water bucket.
Serafina, I'm going to school after all!
Tomorrow Papa is taking me
to live with my aunt in the city.
Papa says Auntie will give me
my own room.
She'll buy me pretty dresses
and we'll have pumpkin soup
and fried pork to eat.
On Sundays, we'll have sweet potato pie
with coconut pudding for dessert!
As soon as I get my new uniform,
Auntie will bring me to school.
Oh, Serafina, I'm so excited!

What aunt? I ask.
Do you know her?

I've never met her,
but Papa says she is lovely.
Papa says she always wanted
a little girl of her own.

Julie Marie's eyes sparkle,
but a shadow
creeps into my heart.

I thought you said your papa
had too many mouths to feed?
Who will help your manman?
Who'll gather firewood,
wash the clothes,
and help care for your brothers?
Who'll help me tend the garden?

Manman said she'll manage.
She wants me to study
and have pretty clothes
and enough food to eat.
And you have your manman
and Gogo to help you in the garden.
Besides, you charmed the peppermint
all by yourself.
You make garden magic—
you don't need me!

Yes I do, I think to myself,
but out loud,
I try to sound happy.

That's wonderful, Julie Marie, I say.

Then I remember my own news.
I'm going to school too,
as soon as the jar is full.
Manman said it herself last night.

Oh, Serafina, I'm so happy!
Julie Marie takes my hand.
I wish Nadia were here.
I wish we could all go
to the same school
and study together!

Her eyes fill with tears.
I'll miss you, Serafina, but now,
we can both be doctors
like we always dreamed.

I push away my sadness
and manage a smile.
Wi! We'll both be doctors
like we always dreamed.

* *
*
*

Early the next morning,
Julie Marie stands in my garden
wearing a clean white dress
that I have never seen before.
Manman says I am prettier
than all the wildflowers
that grow along the hillside.

You are, I say.

She touches her hair.
Manman tucked a kiss
into every twist.

I can see them! I say,
but the laugh
gets caught in my throat
and tears spring into my eyes.

Don't cry, Julie Marie says.
We'll see each other again.
She kisses her hand
and tucks the kiss into my braid.
To help you remember me.

I'll remember you always!

Me too.
I'm only going
to Port-au-Prince.
I'll come home to visit,

and maybe you'll see me
when you come to the city!
Julie Marie smiles.
I promise to think of you
whenever I sing "Uncle Bouki"!

When I sing "Uncle Bouki,"
I promise to think of you too!

We squeeze each other tight.

Prese! Julie Marie's papa
calls from the road.

Julie Marie wipes her eyes
and kisses me on both cheeks.
Look for me when you come
into the city,
she whispers.

Babay, I call, squeezing
the kiss in my braid
and blinking back tears.
Mwen renmen ou.
I love you, my friend.

*

Later that night,
Julie Marie's papa
stops by our house.

I've come to say good-bye, he says.
We're leaving tomorrow before sunrise,
to find work in Saint-Marc.

Saint-Marc! Papa says.
That's quite a distance.
And you've just built a new house.

What about Julie Marie? I ask.

Her papa blinks back tears,
his face stiff and serious.

Serafina, go inside.
Papa's voice is soft,
but his eyes are sharp.
I look down and do as he says.

Manman and Gogo
are counting bunches of basil.
Julie Marie's family is moving
to Saint-Marc! I say.
How can they leave without her?

Gogo touches my face.
To understand the stream, she says,
you must understand the ocean.

※

When my basket is full
of kindling
the next afternoon,
I peek inside
Julie Marie's house.

Nothing is left,
not a pot or a rag,
or a piece of charcoal.

In the open doorway,
a thin-legged spider
drops down and wraps
a sticky web
around a trembling butterfly.

Gogo says, *Never interfere
in nature's dance.*
But I put down my basket,
grab a stick,
and knock away the spider.

The butterfly falls.
Carefully I peel away
the sticky strands
that bind her wings.

The butterfly is so still
I think she's dead.
Gently I brush my fingers
across her body.

Wake up! I whisper.
The butterfly
twitches her wings
and flies away.

Some days, I wish
I could fly away too.

＊

The next day, and the next,
and the next,
Gogo and I pull weeds
and pinch white flowers
from the basil.

Now more will grow,
Gogo says.

This morning Papa took
more of my peppermint
and our biggest green peppers
to Mr. Pétion.
If he thinks they are
good enough
and buys them,
our jar will be full.
I am holding
my breath because
there are only two more days
until school starts!

I snip a few basil leaves
and notice a circle of
small, silvery dots
on the underside of the leaf.
What's this? I ask Gogo.

Gogo frowns
and shakes the plant.
A cloud of tiny

white-winged moths
flies into the air.
We have work to do, Gogo says.
We make a soapy concoction
and wash each leaf.

Whiteflies suck the juices
from healthy plants
and spread disease.
If you let them,
they'll destroy
everything good
and beautiful.

We spend the rest of the afternoon
searching and scrubbing.
I'm worried, but Gogo says,
We just need to keep watch.
We just need to recognize
troublemakers in the garden.

Papa comes home
singing and smiling.

Mr. Pétion bought our peppers
and my peppermint!

Papa adds a handful
of glittering coins to the jar.

At last it is full!

He puts the coin jar
on the floor.
Gogo, Manman,
Papa, and I join hands.
We dance in a circle
around the jar,
and I forget all about
troublemaking whiteflies.

In two days, I will be
going to school!

The next night, Papa brings home
a package wrapped in brown paper
and tied with blue ribbon.
My heart leaps. I tear it open.
Inside is a bright blue uniform,
a white shirt, white socks,
and shiny black shoes.
I hug the crisp, clean clothes
and new shoes to my chest.
Mèsi, Papa! I cry.
Mèsi, Manman! Mèsi, Gogo!

Tears fall down Manman's cheeks.
Don't cry, Manman.
I'll be a good student and make you proud!

Papa beams.
Of course you will, Serafina.

Later, while Manman cooks supper,
Gogo puts coal in an old black iron.
When the iron is hotter than a cooking fire,
she presses away every wrinkle from my uniform.
I carry Gregory outside and look into
his large brown eyes.
Mèsi, baby brother, I whisper.
I promise to make you proud too!
I close my eyes.
Thank you, Baby Pierre!
Thank you, Granpè, for watching over me
and helping Manman to understand.

Gogo is still snoring
when I wake up
and slip out the door
to start my chores.

A thick, long-tailed shadow
brushes across my bare feet.
A gray-masked owl clicks
and flies into the brush.
Crickets chirp, tree frogs chitter.
In the distance, dogs bark,
goats cry, roosters crow.

Everyone is awake to celebrate.

I'm finally going to school!

✳

When I get back,
Papa is leaving for work.
Ou dwe bon! he says.
Be good! Listen to the teacher.

I hug him tight.
I will! I assure him.

Prese! Manman says.
You don't want to be late
on your first day!
She helps me step out
of my green dress
and into my uniform.

Don't put your socks on yet,
Gogo says.
Wait until you get closer
to school so they don't get dirty.

Manman ties bright blue ribbons
in my hair.
I strap Gregory to her back
and help Gogo lift a heavy tin
filled with our best vegetables.
Carefully we put the tin
on Manman's head.
My heart-shaped rock
is in my pocket.
I squeeze it and say a small prayer.
Finally we leave for school!

*
 *
  *

Together we walk
down our hill of dirt and roots,
across a field of rock and grass.
Down one mountain, up another.
Dèyè mòn gen mòn, Gogo says.
Behind the mountains, there are mountains.
We walk and walk.
I can't wait to put on my white socks and
my black shoes made of buckles and shine.
When we finally reach the giant mango tree,
Manman nods.
Time to put on your socks and shoes.

Clouds in the sky
are not softer than the socks on my feet.
Stars in the heaven
are not shinier than my new shoes!

Manman kisses me.
There are tears in her eyes.
Pa pèdi tan! she reminds me.
Don't dawdle!

I promise I won't, I say.

Manman and Gogo wait
as I walk by myself
to the small, square cement building
at the bottom of the hill.

My heart flutters like a butterfly.

*
* *
*

A tall girl with a round face
and a big smile walks toward me.

Alo! Mwen rele Terèz.
What's your name?

Serafina, I say quietly.

Terèz brings me
to a group of girls
jumping rope.

Li rele Serafina, she says
and signals me to jump
into the turning rope.

Now a million butterflies
flutter inside me.

Krick krack, click clack,
the girls chant.
How many coconuts in my sack?
Youn . . . de . . . twe . . . kat . . .

With every count,
a butterfly flutters away.

✳
✳

A skinny bald man
with a gold tooth
shakes a bell
and everyone lines up.

Before we go inside,
the man raises the flag
and the children sing
the same song I heard
on Flag Day.

For our country, for our forefathers,
united let us march.
Let there be no traitors in our ranks.
Let us be masters of our soil.

Today and on special holidays,
we sing in Creole, the teacher says.
But tomorrow we sing in French.
Every day in school, we'll speak French.

Gogo said speaking French
doesn't make you smart,
but Nadia said it does.
Now I'll find out for myself
because I'm going to learn it!

✳

We stay in line
as we walk
into the classroom.
My heart beats
like a bomba drum,
but I look straight ahead
and calmly follow Terèz.

Ahead of me is a big
green board
with yellow writing on it.
The small, blue-painted
cement room
is crowded with rows
of narrow tables
and worn-out benches.
Green notebooks
are piled at the end
of each table.
I think of Nadia
and her yellow notebook.
She was so happy
and proud.
I wonder if she even
goes to school now.

Sit with me, Terèz says,
and I squeeze
into the tiny space
between her and a girl
with a fat bun on her head.

The room smells a little
like dirty laundry,
and the bench is hard as rock.
Already, my shiny shoes
pinch my feet.
But I promised God
if Manman let me go
to school,
I would never complain
about anything again.

Who cares if my shoes
pinch a little?

I'm in school!

✳

The teacher points
to the scribbles on the board.
Monsieur Leblanc, he says.

He signals us
to repeat what he says.

Monsieur Leblanc, we say in unison.
My voice catches in my throat.
What would Gogo say
if she heard me talking French?

The teacher points to himself.
Monsieur Leblanc, he says again.
Je m'appelle Monsieur Leblanc.

Some of the students start
to repeat his words,
but he shakes his head
and waves his hand over the class.
Classe, he says.
Classe, he writes on the board.

He points to himself and repeats,
Monsieur Leblanc.
Again he waves his hand over us.
Classe, he repeats.

Bonjour, classe, he says.
Then with his palms up,
he pulls our voices to him.

Bonjour, Monsieur Leblanc, he says.

Bonjour, Monsieur Leblanc, we repeat.
Our voices rise and fall together.
Bonjour, Monsieur Leblanc.

✳
*   ✳
   *

At lunchtime, we sit outside
on painted wood benches.
Monsieur Leblanc
gives each of us
a scoopful of rice
on a banana-leaf plate.
I eat half and roll the rest
to bring home for Manman.

Boys break into teams
and kick a rag-stuffed sock.
The girls talk
and take turns jumping rope.

When it's our turn,
Terèz and a girl called Romare
let me jump first.
I am so excited to be here
that my heart leaps
higher than my feet.

＊

In the afternoon,
Monsieur Leblanc hands out
the green notebooks
and yellow pencils.

Nadia showed me
how to hold a pencil,
but some of the other students
grab it in their hand
like a maraca.

Monsieur Leblanc walks
around the room
shaking his head
and twisting fingers.

He signals us to
open the notebooks
and copy the lines and circles
that he's written on the board.

Then he walks around the room again,
talking quietly to each student
and writing in their notebooks.

What if he talks to me in French?
I won't know what he's saying.
My heart pounds so hard
I'm afraid it will jump out
of my chest and run away.

When his back is toward us,
Terèz whispers in my ear.
He's just asking your name
so he can write it
on your notebook.

Serafina, I say,
when Monsieur Leblanc
stands over me.
I watch him draw
a neat group
of loops and lines.
When he moves on,
I trace the loops and lines
with my fingers.

Serafina.
My name.
My beautiful,
beautiful name.

*

After school, my new friends
walk one way, and I walk another.
Jean-Pierre,
a boy with a scar over his eye
and a space between his teeth,
follows me up the hill.
Want to see something? he asks.

Manman's voice rolls in my head.
Pa pèdi tan! Don't dawdle!
I keep walking.

Jean-Pierre laughs. *Aren't you curious?*
He offers me a wooden box
decorated with squiggles of paint.
Inside is a small lizard
with a pink beard and no tail.

What happened? I ask.

Jean-Pierre grins and sticks his tongue
in the space between his teeth.
His tail fell off when I grabbed him.

Jean-Pierre!

Don't worry!
Jean-Pierre says. *He'll grow another.*

I hope so!
You need to be gentle with living things!

When I arrive home,
Gogo is in the garden.
Manman stands waiting
in the doorway
with Gregory in her arms.

Manman! School is wonderful!
I have so many new friends—
I step out of my uniform
and continue talking
without stopping—
Terèz, Romare, Bridget, Lesa,
and I forget the others,
but the teacher's name is
Monsieur Leblanc
and he has a gold tooth
and no hair.
Don't tell Gogo,
but we're learning French.
Bonjour, Manman!
And, Manman,
have you ever seen a lizard
with no tail?

Serafina! Manman says.
I want to hear all about school,
but first you need to finish your chores.
There's lots to do!

Gregory coughs
and she pats his back.

I pull out my
soggy banana leaf.
I brought you a present.
If you don't eat,
Gregory won't eat.

Manman shakes her head.
Mèsi, but this is your food.
Gregory coughs again
and she takes the leaf.
Tomorrow you eat.
Now prese!

I try to think only
happy school thoughts,
but angry bees
buzz in my mind.
Doesn't Manman
want to hear everything?
Doesn't she care
about anything but chores?

I wish Julie Marie were here.
I have so much to tell her!
Is her school wonderful
like mine?
Is it crowded?
What color is her notebook?

I think about Nadia again
and wonder where she is.
If she were close,
we could practice French together.

I wonder if Julie Marie is happy
living with her aunt.
I wonder if she's made
new friends.
Does she miss me
as much as I miss her?

Uncle Bouki, Uncle Bouki,
I sing and hope Julie Marie
is thinking of me.

*
* *
*

When I get back,
Gogo is shaking out my uniform
to freshen it.
I work by myself in the garden,
harvesting thyme and checking
for whiteflies.
Banza wanders between
the beans and mint.
He wags his tail and sniffs me.

Bonjour, Banza!
I had such a wonderful day,
even if Manman doesn't want
to hear about it.
I made lots of new friends.
I got a green notebook,
and I am already learning
to write my name!
How was your day?

Banza licks my face
and runs away.

Papa comes home early.
Serafina! he calls.
I run to him.
I've brought a surprise
to celebrate
your first day of school.
He holds up a large,
hairy coconut.

Tell us everything! he says
as he pokes holes in the coconut.

Gogo holds Gregory
while Manman stirs the beans.
We wait for them to cook,
and drink sweet coconut milk.

Wi! Tell us everything,
Manman says.

Sweet, watery juice
dribbles down my chin,
but not into my heart.

I turn to Papa.
*Have you ever seen
a lizard with no tail?*

✳

That night,
when I close my eyes,
I see loops and lines
and turning rope.
I see the first letter
of my name
squiggling like a snake.
I see other letters too,
circles and hooks,
dots and crosses.
But I don't remember
everything.

Tomorrow I'll try harder.
Tomorrow can't come
soon enough!

Bonjour, Monsieur Leblanc!

Bonjour, classe!

I want to see my name again,
but Monsieur Leblanc says that
notebooks don't come out
until after lunch.

Today we start the day by counting.
Monsieur Leblanc taps the board
with a pencil.
Un — deux — trois — quatre — cinq.
Over and over, we recite:
*Un — deux — trois — quatre — cinq —
six — sept — huit — neuf — dix.*

Romare squirms on the bench
beside me.
She turns her hands over,
braids her fingers,
and wiggles them
like they are people sitting
on a bench talking to each other.

Un — deux — trois,
we repeat in singsong voices.

QUATRE — CINQ —
Suddenly Monsieur Leblanc
stands over us,

counting very loud.
He taps our table
and looks at Romare
with dark, sharp eyes.

Six — sept — huit — neuf — dix.

*
✳
*

In the afternoon, Monsieur Leblanc
passes out our notebooks.
We copy letters from the board
and practice writing.

I wish I could take my notebook home
to show Papa, Manman, and Gogo.
But Terèz explains
that we leave them in school
until the end of the school year.
Monsieur Leblanc is afraid
we'll lose them.

Anyway, who has time
to do schoolwork
when we're not in school? Bridget asks.

She is right.
Between gathering water,
working in the garden,
and helping Manman with Gregory,
I hardly have time
to pull out my stethoscope
and play doctor with Banza
when he comes to visit.

But whenever I'm at the ravine,
I always find time
to write my name in the dirt—
S - e - r - a - f - i - n - a.
Now I remember every letter.

*

Each morning, we fold our hands,
and without any pleasant distractions,
repeat the words Monsieur Leblanc
has written on the board.
Le soleil brille. He taps his pencil
in slow rhythm with the words.
Le soleil brille. TAP TAP TAP TAP.
Le soleil brille. The sun shines.

Inside our crowded classroom,
we sit with shoulders touching
while Monsieur Leblanc
TAP TAP TAP TAPs.
Le soleil brille.
The sun shines in French,
the language of our conquerors.

But outside, before school,
Solèy la klere.
When we jump rope
or fly kites,
when we play hide-and-seek,
soccer, or rocks and bones,
Solèy la klere.
When I gather water
or pull weeds,
when I wash clothes,
or sing to my brother,
Solèy la klere.
The sun shines in Creole,
the language of our ancestors.

183

✳

On Tuesdays and Fridays,
Monsieur Leblanc teaches us
about the history of Haiti.

One Tuesday, he tells us
that in 1492
an explorer named
Christopher Columbus
stood on the deck of his ship
the *Santa Maria*.
He saw a beautiful land
with lush green fields
and fruitful mountains.
Christopher Columbus
called the land Hispaniola.

Monsieur Leblanc says Hispaniola
means Little Spain.
He said that the Spanish queen
paid for Christopher Columbus's voyage,
so Christopher Columbus
gave the queen our land.

How, I wonder, *can you give away
something that doesn't belong to you?*

On another Tuesday,
Monsieur Leblanc tells us how
the French conquered the Spanish
and brought slaves
to our flourishing island.

The slaves were forced
to work long hours
on sugar and coffee plantations.

Finally they revolted.

Monsieur Leblanc says the slaves
couldn't read or write,
but they worked together
by sending secret messages
through the honk
of the conch shell
and the beat of a drum.

While he talks,
I remember Gogo's words—
We were slaves, but now we're free.

I think about Granpè
and the Tonton Macoutes.
I'm proud of Granpè
and of Haiti.
I'm proud of our honks
and our drums.
I am thankful
that we are free.

On the second day of November
we celebrate Jou Lèmò,
the Day of the Dead.

As we walk to church,
Gogo reminds me to always honor
our loved ones and our ancestors.
They are never far from us, she says.
Even when we can't see them,
they offer us protection and love.

I think about Granpè and Baby Pierre.
I know they're still close.
They listened to my prayers
and helped me go to school.
I feel them watching me,
caring about me.

I'm happy to have a day
to celebrate their memory.

This year, I also thank
the courageous slaves
who fought for Haiti's freedom.

I ask Baby Pierre
to watch over Gregory
and make his cough go away.

✳

Now is the best time of the year,
Jean-Pierre says.
We are walking together
to the mango tree
like we do every day
after school.
Once November comes,
Christmas is close,
and after Christmas,
there's Independence Day,
and then finally, my favorite,
Carnival!

Jean-Pierre makes me laugh.
The only thing he likes
about school
is playing soccer
and talking about
what he'll do
when he's not in school.
When he grows up,
Jean-Pierre wants to be
a soccer player.

Wow! he says when I tell him
I want to be a doctor.
His eyes bulge.
I never knew a real doctor!

I laugh.
I'm not a doctor yet, I say.

*Well, don't forget me
when you are!* he answers.

We stop at the mango tree
to take off our shoes and socks.

*Did you start making your
Christmas lantern?*
Jean-Pierre asks.

*Christmas is more than
a month away!*

Jean-Pierre grins.
*I know, but it comes quickly,
and I like to make mine fancy.*

*Jean-Pierre, you are
the silliest boy I know!*

✳

On the way home,
I think about last Christmas.

Long after dark,
everyone walked
to Midnight Mass.
Nadia, Julie Marie, me, and
all the children in our village
carried our wooden lanterns,
decorated like little churches.
Nadia had made hers in school,
and it was the prettiest,
with little cutout windows
covered with painted paper
to look like stained glass.

Julie Marie and I
didn't have paint
or fancy paper,
so we covered our lanterns
with leaves and branches
twisted to look like church steeples.

Gogo said it didn't matter
what our lanterns looked like.
*The important thing
is having a place in your hearts
where the Christ Child can rest,* she said.

At Mass, we sang Christmas songs,
and afterward, all the families

walked home together
and visited until
our eyes dropped closed.

This Christmas
will be so different.
Papa has already said
that church is too far away
for us to walk at night.
And Nadia and Julie Marie
and their families
won't be here
to celebrate with us.

But, Papa promised,
we'll find a big branch
to bring inside and decorate.
And we'll save our coins
for a Christmas feast.

Even though this Christmas
will be different,
we still have
Christmas songs to sing,
a Christmas lantern to light,
and our own blessed baby
to celebrate.

A few weeks later,
while we recite our lessons,
we work on our Christmas lanterns.
As we color and paste,
we listen and repeat
whatever Monsieur Leblanc teaches.

Jean-Pierre was right.
Ever since Jou Lèmò,
the days have been flying faster
than a hungry falcon.

Our coin jar is almost full again.
Gogo says some of the coins
are peppermint coins.
Papa says we'll have enough
money to have a Christmas feast.

It's hard not to be happy
at Christmas!
We're already singing carols,
and even Monsieur Leblanc
is smiling.

Jean-Pierre says
when Monsieur Leblanc smiles,
his gold tooth twinkles
like the Christmas star!

✳

Manman is nursing Gregory
when I return from the ravine
the next morning.
I quickly sweep the floor
and empty the chamber pots
before changing into my uniform.

Today, Manman and Gogo
are going to Port-au-Prince,
so we'll walk together
as far as the mango tree.

When I help strap Gregory
onto Manman's back,
I notice a faint rash on his legs
that wasn't there before.

*Manman, did you see
Gregory's legs?* I ask.

Wi, Manman says quietly.
A shadow passes across her face
and Gogo places a bony finger
against her closed lips.

We lift the heavy tin of vegetables
onto Manman's head.

In silence,
we walk down the hills
and across the fields.

When we get to the mango tree,
I put on my white socks and shoes.

Manman and Gogo
follow the road to the city.
I follow the path to school.

Today,
instead of excitement,
only worries
flutter inside me.

Late in the afternoon,
Gogo joins me in the garden.

We had another good day,
she says.
People say your peppermint
is the best in Port-au-Prince.

How is Gregory?
I ask.
Did you make a paste
from water and aloe?

Gogo nods.
It hasn't helped.

How about basil or mint?

Again, Gogo nods.
Serafina, she says gently,
I will tell you
what I told your manman.
Worry is never a cure
for anything.

But—

But we have work to do, Serafina.
Work and prayers and hope.

*
 *
   *

The day before Christmas vacation,
my friends and I hug good-bye.

Jwaye Nwèl!
Merry Christmas!
Merry Christmas!

When we reach the mango tree,
Jean-Pierre reaches into the bag
slung across his back.
I made you a present, he says,
smiling his big-space smile.
He pulls out a crèche made of clay.
Joseph and Mary are a little lopsided,
but the crèche is beautiful.

Mèsi, Jean-Pierre!
This is beautiful,
but I have no gift for you!

Jean-Pierre laughs.
That's okay. I told you
I like to make things.
He smiles shyly.
Jwaye Nwèl, Serafina!
See you next year!

Jwaye Nwèl, Jean-Pierre!
I'm so glad we are friends.

I can't wait to show Manman
my clay crèche
and my Christmas lantern.
The lantern isn't as pretty as Nadia's was,
but it's fancier than last year's.

I step inside our house
with my lantern behind my back.
Manman is bouncing Gregrory
in her arms
while Gogo stirs a cup of tea.

Gregory is crying.

I hide my lantern beneath the table
and place my crèche on the floor.
I'll make him smile, I say.
I take Gregory into my arms
and rock him
while I take a peek at his rash.

It isn't any better,
but it isn't worse either.
I sing my big sister song,
but he only cries more.

Manman dips a cloth into the tea
and puts it in Gregory's mouth.
Shhhhh. Shhhhh, she coos.
Finally Gregory stops crying
and falls asleep.

Manman's eyes are soft and sad.

Don't worry, I say.
Look how round and full
his stomach is.
At least he's not hungry!

Manman smiles at me
and I remember my surprise.
Close your eyes, Manman!
I have a present for you.

Carefully, so as not to wake him,
I hand Gregory to Gogo.
Quietly I pull out my lantern,
then hold it up for Manman.

Okay, Manman,
open your eyes!

It's beautiful, Serafina,
she says.
Her voice is full of warmth
and love,
but her eyes are misty
and sad.

I hurry through my chores.
Papa has promised
that after dinner
we'll decorate
our Christmas branch.

Mr. Pétion and some people in the city
have grand trees, strung
with lights and sparkling ornaments,
but our simple Christmas branch
will be just as special.

The last time she was in the city,
Gogo brought back pretty red berries—
some to eat and some to string
on our branch.
And Manman surprised us
by borrowing colorful buttons
from an old dress
and threading them for us to hang.

While I wait for Papa,
I gather a few sprigs
of white basil flowers
to tuck inside the branches.

This year, we even have our own nativity!
Still, a tiny sadness tugs at my heart.
I wish Gregory's rash would go away.
I wish my friends were here to eat,
sing, and celebrate with us.

✳
✳

Christmas Eve passes
with music, joy,
and my twinkling lantern light.
On Christmas Day,
my belly is so stuffed
with chicken stew
that I know I'll never
be hungry again.
Banza visits me in the garden,
and when I'm sure no one is looking,
I give him a small piece of chicken
that I have tucked in the hem
of my dress.
Jwaye Nwèl, I whisper.

All day, we sing Christmas carols
and Papa tells stories
of when he was a little boy.
I promise that next year
we'll travel to visit Granmè
and Uncle Tomas.
Uncle Tomas tells the best stories!

Gogo and I are still
singing at night when
we wash the dishes,
but Manman is quiet.
Gregory hasn't made any of his
usual peeps and coos.
He keeps his eyes closed
and hardly eats anything.

✳
 ✳
✳

Before I go to bed,
Manman lets me
take Gregory outside.
The moon is only half bright,
but dozens of stars
twinkle in the darkness.
We had a happy Christmas,
didn't we, Gregory? I whisper.
Next year you'll meet
Granmè and Uncle Tomas.
They live in Jacmel, far from here.
I only met them a few times,
but I love them. You will too.
Papa is right.
Uncle Tomas tells the best stories.

Gregory stirs and flutters his eyes.
His lips curve into a small smile.
And then he coughs.
I pat his back and walk him around the house.
Do you see the moon and the stars?
The world is such a beautiful place.
I kiss him softly.
Stay with us, Gregory. Please stay.
There are so many things
I want to teach you.
Please don't leave me, Gregory.
Your big sister loves you,
I start to sing,
but the words get caught
in my throat.

*
* *
  *

The week after Christmas,
Gregory grows
more and more quiet.
His rash is deeper
and darker.
Gogo and I make another paste
from water and aloe.
It soothes him a little,
but he still seems frail.

On January first, we celebrate
the New Year
and Haiti's Independence Day.
At church, I clap my hands,
raise my arms, and pray for
Gregory's rash to heal.
I promise God
to never ask for another thing
if only Gregory can get better.

When we go home,
we celebrate with pumpkin soup.

I tell Manman, Papa, and Gogo
what Monsieur Leblanc
explained to our class.
*Once there were laws that said
only the French could have soup
because they were the ruling class.
But that wasn't fair.
There were lots of laws that*

weren't fair,
so the slaves revolted.
And now, to celebrate,
everybody eats soup.

Papa looks at Manman
and they both smile.

Did you know that Haiti
was the first black republic?
I ask.
Do you know what that means?

That means Granpè
would be proud of you,
Gogo says.

Wi, Manman says.
Granpè would be proud!

Happiness flutters
inside me
and I feel my face
blush with pride.

✳

After the holidays,
everyone seems happy
to be back at school.

Terèz tells us
about her trip to Jacmel,
and Romare tells us
about a new jump rope
she got from Papa Noel.
I can't believe it.
Even Nadia never got a visit
from Papa Noel!

Every time I think of Nadia,
I feel a twinge in my stomach.
I thought she had everything
I wanted.
But now she doesn't have a mother.
I don't even know
if she has a home.
Now *I* have everything.
I wish I could tell her
how sorry I am
that I was jealous.

You look so serious!
Jean-Pierre says.
He smiles.
*Wait till you see
the new house I'm building
for my lizard.*

203

Did his tail grow back? I ask.

Not yet, he says, grinning.
But it will.
Little by little, it will.

The bell rings and we form
our line to go inside.

I wish I could always be cheerful
like Jean-Pierre,
but I can't stop wondering
about Nadia.
I can't stop worrying
about Gregory.

What if he doesn't get better?

*
*
*

My notebook
is beginning to fill
with French words and phrases.

Sometimes I even think
in French.

For some reason,
that makes me sad.

I don't think
knowing French
makes me smarter.
It just means
I know French.

If I were really smarter,
I'd figure out a way
to help Gregory.

The first week
after vacation drags on.
Every day, Monsieur Leblanc
TAP TAP TAPs.

Every day, I worry about Gregory
and hurry home after school,
hoping to find him better.

But every day, he seems the same,
quiet and fragile as a feather.

At night when we wash dishes,
I ask Gogo why we don't take
Gregory to the clinic.

The coin jar is empty, she says.
Red berries, chicken,
and the clinic must wait.

I go to bed early but don't sleep.

It's my fault the coin jar is empty.
It isn't just red berries and chicken.
Every month, we need more coins
to pay for school.

My selfishness
is making Gregory sick.

✳

Monsieur Leblanc
taps the board with his pencil.

Les nuages noirs apportent la pluie.
Black clouds bring rain.

He taps and taps.
Les nuages noirs apportent la pluie.
Les nuages noirs apportent la pluie,
we repeat.

Why am I in school?
I would rather learn
from birds and crickets
than the TAP TAP TAP
of Monsieur Leblanc's pencil.

How will words about weather
help me become a doctor?
How will they help Gregory?

I would rather listen
to Gogo explain
how basil draws the poison
from a bee sting,
or how mint stops the swaying
in a sick stomach.

I would rather
have Antoinette Solaine
show me how to use
the shiny tools
in her black bag.

LES NUAGES NOIRS APPORTENT—
Suddenly Monsieur Leblanc
stands over me.
He taps my table
and looks at me
with sharp eyes.
LA PLUIE.

✻

I love you, I whisper to Gregory
before I leave for school the next day.

All the way to school,
I think about the empty coin jar.
While I lean against the mango tree
to put on my shoes and socks,
I gaze at the road ahead.

I think that if I turned left
instead of right,
I could follow the path
that leads to the clinic
where we took Baby Pierre.
It was a long time ago,
but I remember
the giant mango tree.
It looked just like this one.
I think I would remember the way.

I could find Antoinette Solaine
and she could help
heal Gregory's rash.
I could promise to pay her
with peppermint coins.
Maybe she could teach me
to be a doctor like her.
I could listen
to tiny hearts beating,
instead of the TAP TAP TAP
of Monsieur Leblanc's pencil.

I could learn about medicine
that comes in bottles and tubes,
not just the kind
that grows in our garden.
I could learn how to help people
instead of wasting time
learning silly French words.

From down the hillside,
voices wake me from my daydream—
For our country, for our forefathers—
I'm late!

✳

I tag on the end of the line
and take the only space left,
on the edge of the last bench,
beside Jean-Pierre.

Yesterday's lesson
is still on the board.
Les nuages noirs apportent la pluie.
Black clouds bring rain.

You're late!
Jean-Pierre whispers.

I know! I say.

We sit so close
I smell his sweat
and hear his stomach
grumble.

After school, I climb the hill
with Jean-Pierre.

At the mango tree,
we take off our shoes and socks.
Jean-Pierre walks one way.
I walk the other.

See you tomorrow!
he says.

Above me,
a cloud of black crows
cackles and caws.

In the distance,
a dog howls.

Pa pèdi tan!
Manman always says.

But this one time,
chores can wait.
Besides, if I hurry,
Manman will never know.

*
✳
 ✳
*

I am pretty sure
Antoinette Solaine's clinic
is just down this road.
I'm glad she'll see me
in my uniform.
I'm going to be a doctor
just like you, I'll say.

She'll smile
and maybe she'll ask me
to stay and learn from her.

I'll promise to come back
when I finish my chores.
I'll run all the way home
and not even be late.
I'll tell Manman
that Antoinette Solaine
wants me to be her assistant.
I'll give her the doctor medicine
that Antoinette Solaine says
will cure Gregory.

Where did you see
Antoinette Solaine?
Manman will ask,
smiling and taking
the shiny tube.

She came to my school, I'll say.
She remembered me.

Gogo says that people who lie
are like the whiteflies
that spread poison
in the garden.
People who lie
destroy
everything good
and beautiful.

But Gogo and Manman
don't know everything.
Besides, it will only be
a little lie.
The important thing
is that it will help Gregory.

✳

The road winds and turns
in ways I don't recognize.
Maybe the clinic
is farther
than I remember.

The last time we came,
we were traveling
from a different direction.
Maybe the clinic
is on the other side
of the mountain.

A swarm of whiteflies
flutters in my stomach.

It was a long time ago.
I was only little.
Maybe it was a different
mango tree.

Everything is quiet now.
The crows. The dog.
Everything is silent.

Maybe it was
a different mountain.

＊

Suddenly I recognize
the scent of mangoes,
oranges, and wild thyme.
The grass is speckled
with tiny pink flowers.
Haiti's piece of heaven,
Manman said.

I'm back on the road
that leads to the city!

How did I get here?
Now it will take me
forever to get home.

What will I tell Manman?

✳
* ✳
 *

From nowhere,
crinkling waves
of dry rain
shudder and roll.

Under the earth,
a roaring stampede
rumbles and rushes.

Louder, closer,
LOUDERCLOSER
LOUDERCLOSER
LOU—

A thunderous roar
shatters the sky.
The earth pops, crackles,
and trembles beneath my feet.
A quivering wave
passes through my body.

Manman! I call. *Manman!*

A furious growl
bellows in my ears.
The sky shudders.
The earth shakes.

Manman! I scream and fall
into the trembling grass.

PART

THREE

Around me,
trees sway angrily.
The mountains
heave and moan.
In the sky,
the sun falls
and bounces back.
The earth crumples,
and rolls me
inside its shaking fist.

Moments later,

the trembling stops.

I open my eyes
and lift my head
to a blur
of brown and green.

How long have I been
lying in the grass?

I try to stand,
but a furious roar
still fills my ears.
My stomach sways.

I fall.

Manman! I call again.
But Manman
is far from me.

My mouth fills
with dirt and dust.

Words disappear

inside me.

I close my eyes.

Again, the earth
rocks and trembles.

I clutch the grass
and tense my body.

My ears pound.
My bones throb.

And then,

every

thing

stops.

I stand up,
smooth out
my pretty green dress,
and find
my water bucket
propped beneath
the mango tree
ripe with yellow fruit.

Serafina! Serafina!
Gogo calls.
Serafina, come!

I follow her voice
to the ravine.
Where are you, Gogo?
Where are you?
Tiny stars twinkle
in the cool, clear water.

Suddenly I remember Manman.
Manman is waiting for me.
Manman needs water
to make red beans and rice.

Manman needs water to
bathe Gregory.

I lift my head.

The mango tree is gone.
The yellow fruit,
my bucket,
the clear water,

all gone.

Only a blur
of uprooted trees
and grass.

Only the gritty taste
of dirt
and dusty rock.

Only the fluttering
of whiteflies
in my stomach.

✳

Slowly I pull myself
onto my knees.
My head pounds.
My stomach sways.

I crawl through chunks
of split rock,
torn grass, and
tiny pink flowers.

What happened?

The earth trembles again
and I lay down.

A sour taste
like watery green mango
fills my mouth,
and I throw up dirt and water.

Where am I?

Far away, down the hill,
I hear the sound
of muffled wailing.

✳
* *
*

For a long time,
I lay there,
waiting for the earth
to grow still.

Above the grass,
a tiny yellow butterfly
flutters aimlessly,
like a flower petal
ripped from its stem,
looking for a place to land.

The earth quiets.

I pull myself up.
My arms and knees
burn and bleed.
My uniform is torn
and dirty.

What happened?

The path is gone,
cluttered
with broken stones
and fallen trees.

Is the earth angry
with me
because of my selfishness
and almost-lies?

I look down.
My shoes and socks
are gone, swallowed
by the swaying giant.
My shiny school shoes—
how will I replace them?

Which way do I walk?
How will I ever
find my way home?

*
*
*

Questions whirl and twist
in my mind
like a tangled rat's nest.

Where are Manman,
Gogo, and Gregory?
Did they leave to look
for Papa and me?
Did the angry beast
swallow our home?
Should I stay here or go
to the President's Palace?
If I stay where I am,
will anyone find me?

Softer than a lizard
on a turnip leaf,
I hear Gogo's voice.

If you want your eggs hatched,
sit on them yourself!

✳

I stand up
and slowly step
sideways
down the hillside.

My bare feet slip
on loose dirt
and dry grass.

I'll go to Port-au-Prince.

Papa will be waiting
outside the President's Palace.
Manman, Gogo, and Gregory
will find us there.

✳

Toppled trees stretch across
the path like hungry giants
eager to snatch me
with their knobby limbs,
to trap me
in their tangled roots.

I walk slowly, my legs weak
and trembling.
My heart beats
like a trapped sparrow.
My breath is barely
able to squeeze through
the tightness in my chest.

What have I done?

Again the ground rumbles
and I fall.
The grass I grab on to
pulls from the earth.

I bury my face
in my hands
and wait.

My mouth and eyes
are dry as dirt.
My bruised arms
itch and sting.

I take a deep breath.
Once more,
I drag myself up and walk.
With every step,
my knees buckle and burn.

I keep walking.

The dry grass disappears.
The litter of ripped trees
changes to the litter
of broken cement.

The smell of garbage
and burning wood
chokes me.

Outside their mangled shacks,
mothers and children
stand dazed and crying.

Their frightened faces
swirl around me.
Babbling voices sputter
and snap.

What are they saying?
What are they asking me?

I need to find
my papa.

The soles of my feet
burn and bleed,
but I keep walking.

Finally

I reach the sobbing city.

Through broken streets
and blowing dust,
I straggle and drift.
Surrounded by wails
and walking zombies,
I stagger and limp.

Where is the long iron fence
of the President's Palace?

Papa will be waiting there.
He'll lift me in his arms,
stroke my hair,
and touch my face.
You're safe, Bondye bon,
he'll say.
He'll smell like hard work
and fresh oranges.
He'll laugh
like rolling coconuts.

Manman will cover me
in kisses.
My brave girl, she'll say.
She'll give Gregory
to Gogo to hold,
and hug me tight.
Her hair will smell
like burning charcoal
and garden roots.

The drums will beat gladly
and we'll dance.

I move forward slowly,
looking for my papa,

listening for drumbeats.

The city is filled
with ash, dust,
and open, empty arms.

The air is thick
with smoke, flame,
burning wood, and straw.

Around me,
voices babble and weep.
Sirens scream and wail.

I cover my ears,
but still I hear.

The crowded streets
heave in sorrow.

A heavy dread
slumps inside me.

✳

Where are the fence and path?
Where is the big white church
where we pray on Sundays,
or the supermarket
where Papa sells mangoes,
sweet milk, and rice?

Nothing looks the same.

I keep walking.

In every ash-covered face,
I search for someone
who is searching for me.

Night comes.

I walk beneath
a ragged blanket
of broken sobs
and gray dust.

Underground
the beast rests,
but the earth still shakes
from grief.

Where am I?
Where should I go?

Someone touches
my shoulder.
Long, thin arms
tug at me.

Sleep here, petit mwen.
It's too dark
for wandering.

*

The woman's spindly hands
pat a bare, lumpy mattress.
I lie down.

Above me,
stars weep smoky light.
Beside me,
bony arms keep watch.
Trembling fingers
pray on wooden beads.

I think of Papa
comforting Manman
when the rains came.
Look, he said,
the stars still shine.

Where are you now, Papa?
Where are you, Manman,
Gogo, and Gregory?
Are you looking for me?
Are you hurt?

In the darkness,
my thoughts tumble like
falling stars—

the rising water
and the dead donkey,
Nadia's mother,
Julie Marie,

Granpè,
the Tonton Macoutes,
Baby Pierre, and
Antoinette Solaine—

too many to catch
or follow.

Shipwrecked,
in a throbbing,
mournful sea,
my mattress
floats
toward morning.

✻

Stay with me,
the thin-armed woman says
when daylight wakes me.
Don't wander all alone.

How can I stay?

Manman's words
rustle in my head.
Pa pèdi tan! Don't dawdle.
And Gogo's words—
If you want your eggs hatched,
sit on them yourself.

A siren wails.
The thin-armed woman
turns her head.
I scurry away to look
for Papa's supermarket.

Quickly I'm lost
in mounds of crinkled tin,
mountains of crushed stone,

and a sea of broken people.

✳

Along the street
and on the sidewalk,
between crumbled buildings
and crumpled cars,
people cry
and call for help.

Is Papa one of them?
And Julie Marie—
is she buried beneath
the rubble?
Where are Manman
and Gogo?
Is Gregory safe?

A woman kneels
on the ground
rocking a small
dust-covered baby.
Se lafendimonn! she says.
It's the end of the world.

Is it the end of the world?
Will the beast return
to devour us all?

I kneel down
beside the woman
and gaze at
her quiet baby.
I remember

holding Gregory.
I remember
the rise and fall
of his soft breath.

I remember
my promise
to keep him safe,
and Gogo's soothing words,
Babies are a blessing.

Do blessings hide
beneath a coat of dust?

Gently I brush away
the fine white ash
on the baby's face
and say a prayer.

*

As if to answer me,
a square white car
with dusty tires
and a painted red cross
on the door
pulls up beside us.

A small, wiry woman
with red glasses gets out.
In her hands is a blanket
and a bottle of water.
She stoops down
to look at the baby.
Is he hurt? she asks the woman.
Are you hurt?

The woman shakes her head.
Non! Se pè mwen pè sèlman.
I am only afraid.

We are all afraid, the woman
with glasses says,
but we need to help each other.
She wraps the baby
in the clean blanket
and gives his mother
the bottle of water.
Pa bwè vit. Drink slowly.

Then she looks at my arms
and my knee.

We need to clean your wounds,
she says.

I can't believe it's her.

Words crumble like dirt
in my dry throat,
but I push them out.
Do you remember me?
My name is Serafina.

She looks at my face.

Serafina! Wi!
Of course I remember you!

Antoinette Solaine wraps
her strong, clean hands
around my dirty ones.
Come with me, she says.

Something inside me
swells and shatters.
Tears sting my eyes.

She opens her car door
and helps me crawl inside.
Torn seats prickle my legs,
but the warm smell of coconut
welcomes me.
She pulls a plastic bottle

from a white box behind her seat.
Pa bwè vit, she says,
her voice lilting softly.

Do you know that woman?
she asks.

I shake my head.

*I am going to check on her
and her baby again.
Stay here. I'll be back.*

Cool water glides
across my blistered lips
and dry tongue.

Dr. Solaine, I whisper
when she returns.
Is it the end of the world?

Non! she assures me.
Her brown eyes are soft
like water from the ravine.
Her voice is as gentle
as the mourning dove.
Youn tranbleman tè, she says.
An earthquake.

She climbs in beside me,
pulls a cloth from her bag,

wets it, and cleans my wounds.
Even though they burn,
I stay very still and
watch how she works,
so tender and calm.
These aren't so bad, she says.
You were very lucky.

I manage a smile.

She strokes my cheek
and puts her bag
on the seat behind us.
Then she stretches
her right arm
to protect me,
as she slowly, carefully,
steers her car
onto the crowded road.

Our clinic was spared, she says.
So I came here,
where I can be more helpful.

Youn tranbleman tè.
An earthquake.

Even the word
makes me shudder.

*

Antoinette Solaine
eyes my dusty uniform
and smiles.
I see you go to school,
she says gently.
Do you live in the city now?
Is your school here?

Words stick in my throat
like sharp stones.
How can I tell her
that my school is outside the city,
and that school is not how
I thought it would be?
That I don't want to sing
and count in French,
I want to learn medicine!
That I was looking for *her*
and got lost?
How can I tell her
about the almost-lies
that tumble inside me
like whiteflies?

I look out the window.
My school isn't in the city, I say.
I only came here to look for Papa.
Whenever there's trouble,
he meets us at the President's Palace.
But the palace is gone!
I looked, but I can't find it.

Antoinette Solaine reminds me of Papa.
She just listens
and doesn't ask too many questions.
I keep talking.
Manman and Gogo were home
waiting for me to return from school
when the earthquake came.
We have a new house now,
hidden in the hills, far from the city.
We moved when the flood
washed away our old house.
It's quiet there, with lots of space.
We even have a garden.
Well, we had a garden. . . .

Antoinette Solaine's voice
is soft as honey.
The worst earthquake damage
is here in the city
and neighboring villages.
Your manman and Gogo should be safe.

The tightness in my chest
opens and I breathe deeply.
I have a new brother too, I say.
His name is Gregory.
He's sick.
I was looking for you
when the earthquake came.

Antoinette Solaine's eyes

widen and glisten.
What's wrong with him?

I tell her about the rash,
how it spread and makes him cranky.
I tell her about the paste
Gogo and I made of aloe and water,
how it soothed him
but didn't make him better.
His belly is round and full,
so I know he isn't hungry.
I don't know what's wrong with him.

Sometimes even when we eat,
Antoinette Solaine says,
our bodies are hungry.
Has his skin become scaly?

No.

Is his hair falling out?

I shake my head.

Is he still eating some?

I nod.

Then it is not too late. . . .
We'll find your brother, she says,
and if I can help him, I will.

*
* *
*

Dr. Solaine's car moves
slower than a turtle.
Every inch, I scour the crowd
for Papa.

A woman with a red bandanna
wrapped around her mouth and nose
hangs on the shoulders
of an old man in a torn shirt.

A scrawny girl with wide,
frightened eyes
leans against a mound of rubble.
One hand clutches a yellow cookie.
The other grips her shoulder.
The girl's lips are white
with dust.
Her loose braids
and even her eyelashes
are white with dust.
But under them,
I see two gentle eyes,
dark and shiny
as the seeds
of the sapote fruit.

Could it be?

✳
✳

Julie Marie! I call.

Antoinette Solaine
stops the car.
*Do you see someone
you know?*

Wi! My friend!
I open my door
and run to her.
*Julie Marie!
It's me, Serafina!*

The girl wraps her arms
tighter around herself.

*Julie Marie! Is it you?
Don't you remember me?*

Antoinette Solaine kneels
beside her and talks calmly.
We're here to help. You're safe.

Uncle Bouki, Uncle Bouki,
I sing quietly.
My voice is low and cracked.
*Are you sleeping?
Are you sleeping?*

*
*
*

Julie Marie looks up.
Serafina?
Is it really you? she whispers.
She stretches her leg
and a river of blood oozes.

We need gauze! I say.

There's a roll in my black bag.
Bring it here!
And the small roll of tape.

I race to get them.
I can lift her leg while you wrap it,
I say, and Antoinette Solaine nods.
Gently, carefully,
I hold Julie Marie's foot
high enough above the ground
for Antoinette Solaine
to reach under it.
'Round and 'round she wraps the gauze.
Julie Marie winces and closes her eyes.
Ou dwe brav, I whisper.

Antoinette Solaine carries Julie Marie to her car
and places her in the backseat.

Mèsi, Manman, Julie Marie says,
her eyes still closed.
I knew you would come.
I knew you would look for me.

∗
 ∗
 ∗

We drive past a village
of sheets and sticks,
past rooms
of flattened cardboard boxes.

So many walking people.
Where are they going?
The earth stopped moving,
but they cannot.

I turn to Antoinette Solaine.
Where are we going? I ask.

*I'm bringing you and Julie Marie
someplace safe,* she says.

But what about my papa?

Antoinette Solaine smiles.
*Let's get you and Julie Marie
taken care of—
then we'll see about your papa.*

My papa.
*Where are you, Papa?
Where are you?*

✳

I can see your heart is full
of compassion and kindness,
Antoinette Solaine says as we drive.
You would make
a wonderful doctor.

My heart swells.
But being a doctor means
staying in school, I say.

Antoinette Solaine smiles.
Wi! Don't you like school?

I like learning to write.
And I like listening to stories about Haiti.
But I don't like learning French!
Why can't we learn in Creole?
Then everyone could understand each other.
How does learning French help people?

Antoinette Solaine laughs.

Those are good questions, Serafina!
You have a clever mind.

We are both quiet for a moment.
Antoinette Solaine glances
in the car mirror, then looks ahead
and turns a corner.

I'll tell you a secret, she says.
Learning French was not easy
for me either.
People in my village
spoke only Creole.
But I wanted to be a doctor
so I studied hard.

She smiles.
Maybe someday,
when you're grown-up,
you can help change things
so that children will learn
in their own language.
But for now,
we must deal with things
as they are.
We must not let
learning French
stand in the way
of helping people.

* *
* *

We arrive at a white tent.
A group of people
sing softly.
Bondye bon, Bondye bon.
God is good.

Antoinette Solaine stops the car
and looks at me.

Promise me you'll stay in school, Serafina.
You have a smart mind.
Haiti needs people like you.
People who believe in us,
who respect our culture
and our language.
She smiles.
If you stay in school,
I'll let you come to the clinic
and help me
when things are normal again.
But right now, she says,
taking a deep breath,
right now there's work
to be done here.

My head and heart are racing.
Antoinette Solaine thinks
I have a smart mind.
She thinks Haiti needs people
like me.

Imagine helping her!
Imagine working at the clinic!

And then my
rising heart sinks.
Will things ever again
be normal?

Will there ever again
be ordinary days
of gathering water,
and working in the garden,
of going to school,
and caring for Gregory—

of waiting for my papa
to come home?

Antoinette Solaine
lifts Julie Marie
and carries her inside
the white tent.
A woman with gray eyes
and a long gray braid
rushes over.

Antoinette! she says. *You're safe!*

Wi! Mèsi Bondye,
there was no damage to the clinic.
She nods at Julie Marie and me.
I've brought two friends.

The woman with the gray braid smiles.
Are you hungry? she asks.

Antoinette Solaine
sits Julie Marie down
in a corner of the tent.
Her friend brings
two bowls of rice.
The rice fills my belly,
but Manman's rice
tastes better.

✳

I'll come back for you
as soon as I can,
Antoinette Solaine says.
She tugs at my chin.
We'll look for your papa,
I promise.

Thank you, I say
and wish there were words
big enough
to hold all my gratitude.
Thank you for everything.

Antoinette Solaine looks
into my eyes,
then pulls me close
and hugs me.
You're welcome, Serafina,
she whispers.
You are
a very brave little girl.

✳

Julie Marie and I hold hands.
We listen to the soft singing
of the people outside the tent,
the muffled cries and groans
of the people inside.

Where is your aunt?
I finally ask.
Was she hurt
in the earthquake?

Julie Marie turns her head.
I don't know, she mumbles.
Where were you?
Is your manman all right?

Is Julie Marie
hiding something?

I think so,
but I'm not sure, I say.
Whiteflies flutter
in my stomach.

Can Julie Marie tell
I am hiding something?

✳

After a long while,
Julie Marie says,
I ran away from her.
She wasn't my real aunt.
Papa only said that
so I wouldn't be afraid.
She told him
she would buy me clothes
and send me to school
and care for me,
but she lied.
She only wanted me
to cook and clean.
And when I asked about school,
she beat me.

A tear rolls down Julie Marie's cheek.
I want to go home.
I want to see my family.

I think about all the lies
I almost told to Manman.
I think about Julie Marie's family
gone to Saint-Marc.
I can't bring myself to tell her.
Is that the same as lying?

I want to go home too, I say.
We huddle close and close our eyes.
Darkness is our ragged bedcover,
drifting voices our mournful lullaby.

✳

Morning shouts
wide and white
like an open coconut.
I stretch my legs,
but my bones hurt
to move.
Leve, Julie Marie,
I say, shaking her gently.
How is your leg?

Julie Marie rubs her eyes.
It was better when I was sleeping.
She stretches her arms and winces.
Bonjou, Serafina.

All around us, men and women
in white coats and worried faces
skitter like captive mice.
We don't see
Antoinette Solaine
or the woman with the gray eyes
and the long gray braid.

Julie Marie, I whisper,
I'm leaving to look for my papa.

Non! Don't leave me!

Shhhhh! Only for a while.
I promise I'll come back.
Now you need to rest.

Away from our shelter,
the air sags with the smell
of sweat and garbage.

Even my own self smells.
Rotten vegetables
and spoiled fruit
do not stink
as much as me.

I wish I were in the garden
with the sweet scent
of soil, basil, and thyme.

Are Manman and Gogo
in the garden?
Or are they here in the city
looking for me and Papa?

In every passing face,
I search for them.

✷

In the daylight,
the city seems
less strange.
I pass a mountain
of blue dust
and recognize
the crumbled walls of the cafe
Papa and I passed
on our way
to his supermarket.
I know I'm close
when I see colored umbrellas.
They lie tangled together
like a broken rainbow.

Gogo says rainbows
remind us
of the friendship between
heaven and earth,
the strength
of different colors
stitched together.

But what about
a broken rainbow?
What do its gnarled
and twisted colors say?

✳

I look around me.
Everything is crumbled.
Everything is mangled or crushed.

Papa would never leave me
so lost and wandering.

Papa would lift the earth
and pull down the heavens
to search for me.

Is he searching for me now,
worrying that I was swallowed
by the angry beast?

A black cloud wraps around me.
Did the beast swallow him?

My mind drifts
to the darkest place.

Without Papa,
who will hold my hand
and twirl me through the city streets?
Who will bring me sweet surprises
like sugarcane and coconut?

Without Papa,
who will tell Manman
that children must dance and play
even when there are chores to do?

Without Papa,
no singing or laughter
will bellow through the hillside.

The world will be silent,

empty,

broken.

Around me, people crawl
on hands and knees,
looking for those they love.
They scratch and paw
like hungry animals,
searching for food.

Are people still trapped?
Are people still alive?
Could Papa be trapped?
Could Papa be alive?

It hurts to bend,
but I crawl on my knees.
I scratch and paw,
not caring how I look or sound.
Papa! Papa! I call.
I kneel beside
the broken rainbow.
It's me, Serafina.

No answer.

I crawl to the crumbling
pink walls
around the corner.
Papa, I call.
Are you there, Papa?

Again, no answer.

✳

I stand and start walking.
The wound on my knee
begins to ache.

Papa! Papa! It's me, Serafina,
I call to the empty dust.

People walk by me like zombies.

It's me, Papa, are you here?

The black cloud tightens around me
until I can hardly breathe.

Papa, please hear me!
It's me, Serafina.

I stop and lean against
a mangle of silver and wood.
I press my hand against my knee
and in looking down,
I see a small scrap of burlap
tangled in the silver.

A small scrap of burlap
between wood from a barrel
and silver from a shopping cart.

I must be at
Papa's supermarket!

✳
* ✳
*

I fall to my knees again.

Papa! Papa! I call.
It's me, Serafina!
Papa!
Papa, are you here?

Back and forth,
I scrabble and call.

Papa! Papa!

But there is only

silence,

emptiness,

sorrow.

✳

I lean against
the mangled carts,
wrap my arms
around my legs,
and cry.

Ede mwen, a voice calls,
so quietly I barely hear it.

Ede mwen.

I stop crying.

Am I dreaming?

Papa?
Is that you?

Serafina? the voice says.

Wi, Papa! Se mwen!
I paw and dig,
pull and push.

Papa! Papa!
I scream,
and feel myself
lifted like an angel.

✻

Dozens of dusty brown hands
claw, pull, and beg Papa
to hold on.

I close my eyes and pray.
Hold on, Papa,
please hold on.

Dozens of dusty brown hands
pound, smash,
and sweep away
the massive stone.

I watch and pray.
Please, God,
please help Papa to hold on.

Rock by rock,
pebble by pebble,
bare, blistering hands
dig, beg, and promise.
Kenbe fò! Hold on!
We'll get you out!

The sun draws higher
and hotter,
lower
and cooler,
but the faithful brown hands
never stop moving.

Papa's leg is trapped
behind a slab of cement
too large to move.

What if they can't
free him?
What if the earth
rumbles again?
What if the wall
crumbles down on him?

Please, please, please, God,
I pray.
Please keep my papa safe!
I promise I'll never
wander away
or tell another lie—
ever again!

Finally joyous shouts
chime like church bells.

He can move his legs!
Pull him out slowly!
Dousman! Be gentle!

I don't know how many
minutes, hours, days pass,
but at last my papa is free!

He lies on his back,
smiling.
Mèsi! Mèsi!
he says to the joyous,
clapping crowd.

He slowly bends his leg,
and a man with a light
on his helmet helps him
to stand.

Papa's eyes
search for me.

I push through the crowd.
Papa! Papa! I cry,
and everyone cheers
as I run to him.

✳

Papa wraps
his strong arms around me.
Serafina! he whispers.

Papa, I cry into his
torn, dirty shirt.
Papa! Papa!

Every other word
is lost to us.
Every other thought
or prayer is lost.

I smell his sweat,
the dust of his waiting.
I feel his heart thumping—

Bom-bom
Bom-bom
Bom-bom

Finally Papa pulls away.
Gently he touches my face.
Manman? he whispers.
Gogo? Gregory?

I look down.

Papa, I don't know.

✳

Papa's confused eyes
pierce the darkness
gathered inside me.

All my broken promises,
my almost-lies and mistakes,
all my sadness and my fears
rise and explode
in great waves
of sorry tears.

I should have gone straight home
after school. I thought I knew
where I was going but it
was a different mango tree
so I got lost
but not really lost because I was
on the road to the city.

Serafina! Papa says. *Slow down.*

I take a deep breath.
I just wanted to ask Antoinette Solaine
what to do for Gregory's rash
because Gogo's herbs aren't working
and it's my fault
we don't have enough coins
to take him to the clinic.
But the earthquake came
and I thought you would be waiting
by the President's Palace

*but the palace isn't there, Papa,
and I lost my shoes but they hurt
my feet. Even in school they hurt
and I can't always concentrate
on what Monsieur Leblanc says.
Mwen regrèt sa!*

I should have gone straight home.

✳

Papa holds me so tight
that the waves stop pushing.
You didn't go right home
after school?

No, Papa. Mwen regrèt sa.
I am so, so, so sorry.

Manman trusted you.
She needed you.

My heart shrinks in shame.
Mwen regrèt sa.

We need to find her.

Papa, I saw Antoinette Solaine.
She said the earthquake damage
is mainly here in Port-au-Prince
and the homes closest to the city.
She said our house is most likely safe.

Mèsi Bondye, Papa says,
closing his eyes.

When he opens them,
he just looks at me
and doesn't say anything.

He knows I betrayed Manman's trust—
and his.

How will he ever forgive me?

Serafina, he says,
his hands gripping
my arms.

Before he can speak,
I tell him
through my tears
over and over again
how sorry I am.
I know I should have gone
straight home.

Serafina, he says softly,
his eyes
searching mine.
If you had,
I never would have
survived.

You looked for me.
You didn't give up.

You saved my life.

We hold each other
for a long time.
I feel Papa's shoulders tremble.
You're safe, Papa,
I whisper. *Bondye bon.*

Bondye bon,
I think to myself.
God really is good.
God took my mistake
and made a miracle.

Papa, I whisper.
I found Julie Marie too.
She's in the hospital tent.
I promised I'd go back for her.
Her leg is badly hurt.

I tell him about Julie Marie's aunt,
who wasn't really her aunt.
Now Julie Marie is all alone.
Can't we take her home with us?
I'll share my rice with her,
and we can work together in the garden,
and help Manman,
and sell more peppermint.

Papa takes my hand and we walk
back to the white tent.
If she can be moved, he says,
we'll take her with us.

✳

Outside the tent,
people with empty buckets
line up to gather water gushing
from a large white truck.
Eskize mwen, eskize mwen.
Excuse me, Papa says,
as we limp into the tent.

Serafina! Over here!
Julie Marie sits
on a long table,
her leg stretched out
in a clean white bandage.
You found your papa!
she exclaims.
She gives him
a wide smile
and he hugs her.

The woman with
the gray eyes appears
holding two bottles of water
and four packages of biscuits.
This is my papa, I say,
and my heart bursts with joy.
She smiles and hands us
the water and biscuits.
You left before breakfast,
she says to me.

Mèsi! Is Julie Marie

strong enough
to come with us?

Her leg was badly slashed
but not broken.
Others are much worse.
If your papa carries her,
she'll be fine.

Papa lifts Julie Marie in his arms.
Just as we are leaving,
Antoinette Solaine appears.
Serafina! she calls.

I found my papa! I blurt out
and she smiles at us both.

You have a brave daughter,
she says to Papa.

Papa nods and smiles at me.
Wi. My brave Serafina.
Thank you for keeping her safe.

Antoinette Solaine looks at me
and shakes two small bottles.
These vitamins are for Gregory.
She opens the bottle
and shows me
how to squeeze the dropper
so that the liquid rises inside.

Just up to this line.
And just once a day.
And this is a cream for his rash.
Again, just once a day
will be enough.

Then she asks Papa
exactly where our new house
is located.
He tells her and
she promises to visit
as soon as she is able.

Remember what
we talked about, Serafina.
Think about what I said.
We need you.

I smile and nod.

Mèsi, Papa says.
Mèsi, Julie Marie and I repeat.

Together, the three of us
leave the white tent
to make our way home.

✳

The heavy smell of sweat
and sorrow choke me,
but gratitude and hope
spin a sheltering cocoon.

Twilight begins to burn
the corners of day.

Slowly Papa, Julie Marie, and I
wobble through the ruins.

People stop moving
and begin to make
small shelters
from sheets and shirts
draped over crushed fences
and steel posts.

I want to keep walking,
but Papa shakes his head.
*The journey will be too long
and difficult
without daylight to guide us.*

We have no sheets
and only the thin, sweaty
shirts on our backs.
Papa offers a family
a package of biscuits
in exchange for a large,
flattened cardboard box.

He sets Julie Marie down.
I snuggle close beside her,
making room for Papa too.

I'll be right back, Papa says.

He leaves to help a family
drape a torn sheet
over three large sticks.

Sheets and sticks don't make
a very strong home,
but sometimes neither do
wood and cement.
I watch Papa's arms stretch
wide and strong
against the darkening sky.

The only unbreakable home
is one made from love.

✳

Julie Marie closes her eyes.
Let's hurry and sleep.
Tomorrow I'll see my family.

I remember my promise
to always be truthful.

Julie Marie, I whisper,
I need to tell you something.

She opens her eyes and smiles.
You like to talk when I like to sleep.

I push the words out quickly
so I won't lose my courage.
Your family moved away.

Julie Marie's face crumples.

After you left, they left too.

I don't understand.

After you left, your papa
came to tell us
that your family
was going to Saint-Marc
to look for work.

The weight of our sadness mingles
with the deepening dusk,
and neither of us speaks.

Then, suddenly,
Julie Marie's face brightens.

That's good news, Serafina!
Saint-Marc is far from here.
Very far.
Now I'm sure my family
is well and safe!
But, Serafina—my leg—
where will I stay
until I'm strong again?

I squeeze Julie Marie's hand.
Papa says you can stay with us!
I'll take care of your wound,
and when you're well again,
we can both work in the garden
and help Manman.

Can your papa get word
to my family—
to let them know that I'm safe?
Manman must be worried.

Of course, I say.

What about school?
Julie Marie asks.
You haven't told me
about school.
Remember, you promised
to teach me
everything you learned.

And I will! I say.
Learning French
to become doctors
seems silly,
but for now that's what
we need to do.
You can practice
while your leg heals.
I tell Julie Marie
what Antoinette Solaine said
about helping in the clinic.
Maybe you can help too.

Someday we really will be doctors,
Julie Marie says.
If we don't lose hope,
it will happen.

Wi! Wi! I say, feeling
the truth of that in my heart
and remembering my promise
to honor Granpè and his dream.

✳
✳

Maybe someday we'll find Nadia too,
Julie Marie says.

An old sorrow and shame
burn in my stomach.
When I saw Nadia at the parade,
I confess, *I pretended I didn't.*
I used to be jealous of her.

Julie Marie nods.
I know, she whispers.

But you never were.
How come?

Manman says everyone
has their own path.
And everyone's path
has both flowers and thorns.

Your manman is right, I say.
I wish I could tell Nadia
that I'm sorry.
I wish I could tell her
how pretty she looked in her
yellow uniform.

Maybe one day you will tell her,
Julie Marie says.
Maybe one day we will find her.

*Wi! The important thing
is to never give up.*

Julie Marie winces and rubs her leg.

You should rest, I say.
*If you want to get better,
you need to rest.*

Julie Marie laughs.
*You already sound like a doctor.
I will rest if you stop talking!*

Papa comes back.
Go to sleep, Serafina,
he whispers as he lays down.
It's been a long day.

I rest my head on his chest.
Through his damp shirt,
I hear his heart beat softly.

Bom-bom
Bom-bom
Bom-bom

In the distance,
someone plays the drums.

Bom-bom
Bom-bom
Bom-bom

People sing quietly.
Bondye bon.
Bondye bon.
God is good.

Already Julie Marie
has fallen asleep.
Before long, Papa snores
in rhythm with the drums.

I close my eyes.
I thank God
for keeping my friend
and my family safe.

Tonight the stars
dangle and dance clearly.

Was it just three days ago
that I kissed Manman good-bye
and Monsieur Leblanc stood
tapping at my table?

Was it just three days ago
that the rumbling earth
shattered our world?

I think about Jean-Pierre
and pray
that he is somewhere safe.
I think about Julie Marie,
happy and hopeful even after
everything she suffered,
and about Nadia and Papa,
Manman and Gregory,
how everyone's path
has both flowers
and thorns.
I think about Antoinette Solaine
and her black bag,
about Gogo and her herbs.

I wonder about all the people
wandering in the ruins—

the bony woman who kept watch
while I slept—did I thank her?

The woman and her
dust-covered baby—
are they safe?

There are so many lost
and broken people.
How can we help them all?

Softer than the rustle
of spider's silk,
Manman's voice
echoes in my mind.

Ou dwe brav, Serafina.
Life is hard,
but no matter what happens,
we beat the drum
and we dance again.

* * *

I reach into my pocket
and wrap my fingers
around my heart-shaped rock.
Dust and debris are everywhere,
but in my hand,
my heart-shaped rock is still
smooth and firm,
unchanged by the earthquake.

Nothing is stronger than love,
Manman said.
In my mind, I see her
stirring rice and plucking bugs.
I think about her
growing up without a papa—
how scared she must have been
when the Tonton Macoutes
took him away!
How scared I was
when I thought
I'd lost *my* papa.

I think of all Manman's worries
hovering like mosquitoes,
making her brittle and jumpy.
I think of her carrying me
in the flood,
lifting me high
above the water,
even though
I was mad at her.

Sometimes buzzing bees
stay too long
in our brains,
but only because
we let them.

Tomorrow
when I see Manman,
I'll hug her tight.
I'll help her sift
through the rice,
and tell her
how much I love her.
I'll help her understand,
I *am* happy
with what I have,
but so many people
have nothing.
I only want
to help them.

In the growing darkness,
voices lower,
but the drums beat
soft and steady.

Above me,
stars still shine.

✳

HAITIAN CREOLE
ALPHABET AND PRONUNCIATION GUIDE

The Haitian Creole alphabet has twenty-nine letters. Each letter in a word is pronounced, and the last syllable of a word is usually the one that is stressed.

LETTER	PRONUNCIATION
a	short *a* sound as in *apple*
an	short *a* with nasal tone
b	same as English
ch	*sh* sound as in *share*
d	same as English
e	long *a* sound as in *play*
en	short *e* sound with nasal tone
è	short *e* sound as in *fed*
f	same as English
g	same as English
h	*ch* as in *chop*
i	*ee* as in *feed*
j	*s* sound as in *treasure*
k	same as English
l	same as English
m	same as English
n	same as English
o	long *o* sound as in *hope*
on	long *o* with nasal tone
ou	*oo* sound as in *school*
ò	*aw* sound as in *paw*
p	same as English
r	same as English
s	same as English
t	same as English
ui	*oo-ee* sound as in *Louie*
v	same as English
w	same as English
y	same as *y* in *yellow*
z	same as English

GLOSSARY OF
FOREIGN PHRASES

Words and phrases are Haitian Creole. Those noted with an asterisk (*) are French.

Ale lwen (AL-e lWEN) — Go away

Babay (bye-BYE) — Good-bye

Bondye bon (bon-DJAY bon) — God is good

Bonjou (BON-zure) — Hello

*Bonjour (bohn-ZURE) — Hello

Bwa sèch (BWA sesh) — Literally, dry wood. But when used as the response to tim tim, it signals the storyteller to begin

Dèyè mòn gen mòn (deh-yeh moan gay-EN moan) — Behind the mountains, there are mountains

Dousman (DOOS-man) — Be gentle

Ede mwen (eh-DEH mwen) — Help me

Eskize mwen (es-KEEZE mwen) — Excuse me

Granmè/Granpè (gran-MEH/gran-PEH) — Grandma/Grandpa

*Je m'appelle (jhuh ma-PEL) — My name is

Jou Lèmò (joo le-MO) — Day of the Dead

Jwaye Nwèl (jwa-yay nWELL) — Merry Christmas

Kenbo fò (KAN-be foe) — Hold on

*Le soleil brille (lulh so-LAY breel) — The sun shines

*Les nuages noirs apportent la pluie (lay noo-ahjh nwahr ah-PORT la ploo-ee) — Black clouds bring rain

Lespwa fè viv (lespwa FEH veev) — Hope makes us live

Leve (lay-VYAY) — Get up

Li rele (lee ray-LAY) — His/her/its name is

Manman (MON-mon) — Mom, mama

Mèsi anpil (mehsee an-PEEL) — Thank you so much

Mwen dwe travay (mwen dway trav-EYE) — I have work to do

Mwen pè (mwen peh) — I'm scared

Mwen regret sa (mwen ray-GRET sa) — I'm so sorry

Mwen renmen ou (mwen rain-MAIN oo) — I love you

Non mwen se (NON mwen say) — My name is

Ou dwe bon (oo DWAY bon) — Be good

Ou dwe brav (oo DWAY brav) — Be brave

Ou se zanmi mwen (oo say zan-MEE mwen) — You're my friend

Pa bwè vit (pa BWEH veet) — Drink slowly

Pa pèdi tan (pa pehz-DEE ton) — Don't dawdle

Petit mwen (pee-TEET mwen) — My child

Prese (pray-SAY) — Hurry

Se lafendimonn (say la-fen-dee-MOAN) — It's the end of the world

Se pè mwen pè sèlman (say peh MWEN peh sel-MON) — I am only afraid

Solèy la klere (so-LEH-y la kleh-RAY) — The sun shines

Swiv mwen (sweev mwen) — Follow me

Tim tim (teem teem) No literal translation . . . simply a playful invitation to guess a riddle

Wì (wee) — Yes

Youn tranbleman tè (yoon tron-blay-MON teh) — An earthquake

ACKNOWLEDGMENTS

I gratefully acknowledge all those whose support and encouragement helped create this book.

Thank you to the librarians at Starr Library in Rhinebeck, New York, and at St. Thomas Aquinas College in Sparkill, New York, who made sure I received my research material in a timely manner. Thanks to Pierre and Terry Leroy from the Haitian People's Support Project, a not-for-profit organization supporting the people of Haiti since 1990. Despite their busy schedules, Pierre and Terry welcomed me into their home and introduced me to Professor Denize Lauture. Professor Lauture was an invaluable resource in helping me understand and appreciate the subtleties of Haitian language and culture. My respect for Professor Lauture and for the people of his beloved country is enormous. *Mèsi anpil!*

Thank you to my agent, Jodi Reamer, for her continued advice, and to Emellia Zamani from Scholastic, who always answers my questions promptly and cheerfully. Thanks also to my copy editor, Monique Vescia, and book designer, Marijka Kostiw. My heartfelt thanks to Sean Qualls (from my beloved Brooklyn) for his sensitive and creative cover art. You truly captured the heart of *Serafina's Promise*! Deepest gratitude to my wonderful editor, Tracy Mack, who consistently challenges my characters and keeps them from wandering too far from their paths. I am so lucky to work with you!

As always, I am most grateful for my family. Thanks to SB, my faithful walking and writing companion, and to Marc, Celia, and Alex—who remind me every day that nothing is stronger than love.

FOR ROSEMARY AND THERESA

MY SISTERS, MY FRIENDS

✳

LIBRARY OF CONGRESS CATALOGING-IN-PUBLICATION DATA AVAILABLE

ISBN 978-0-545-53564-9

10 9 8 7 6 5 4 3 2 1   13 14 15 16 17

Printed in the U.S.A.   23
First edition, October 2013

The text type was set in Adobe Garamond Pro.
The title type was hand-lettered by Sean Qualls.
The display type was set in Adobe Garamond Pro.
Book design by Marijka Kostiw